...e Thompson

returns to Harlequin Blaze in 2012

with more

Sons of Chance

Chance isn't just the last name of these rugged Wyoming cowboys—it's their motto, too!

Saddle up with

#687 Long Road Home
(June 2012)

#693 Lead Me Home
(July 2012)

#699 Feels Like Home
(August 2012)

And don't forget about the ebook prequel,

Already Home

(Available in May 2012)

Take a chance...on a Chance!

Dear Reader,

I'm no gourmet cook. In fact, not long ago while cooking for friends, I attempted to make green beans with almonds in a baking dish with a glass lid. As I lifted the lid to check the doneness (that's a technical term known only to experienced chefs), I dropped the lid, which shattered into the beans. My dear guests ate the beans while picking out bits of glass.

Therefore, when I wrote about Aurelia Imogene Smith working away in the Last Chance Ranch kitchen preparing fancy French dishes with ingredients I couldn't pronounce, you know I was living in a fantasy world. But what's a fantasy without a cowboy, I ask you? So I brought Matthew Tredway, master horse trainer, right into that ranch kitchen to meet Aurelia.

We've all been told that the way to a man's heart is through his stomach. Must be true, because in no time Aurelia finds her way into Matthew's heart, but she also manages to lure the rest of him, too. And I have to say, in the interest of full disclosure, that food isn't the only thing Matthew is interested in.

If you've been a faithful reader of the Sons of Chance series—and I hope you have!—you may wonder what Aurelia's doing in a kitchen normally dominated by ranch cook Mary Lou Simms. Turns out that Mary Lou and Watkins, the ranch hand who was sweet on her, finally decided to tie the knot and are off on their honeymoon.

If that's news to you, you need to come on out to the Last Chance, sip a cup of coffee on the porch, and catch up on the doings there. I know you wouldn't want to miss a single thing!

Lipsmackingly yours,

Vicki

Vicki Lewis Thompson

LEAD ME HOME

HARLEQUIN®
entertain, enrich, inspire™

Recycling programs
for this product may
not exist in your area.

ISBN-13: 978-0-373-79697-7

LEAD ME HOME

ABOUT THE AUTHOR

New York Times bestselling author Vicki Lewis Thompson's love affair with cowboys started with the Lone Ranger, continued through Maverick and took a turn south of the border with Zorro. She views cowboys as the Western version of knights in shining armor—rugged men who value honor, honesty and hard work. Fortunately for her, she lives in the Arizona desert, where broad-shouldered, lean-hipped cowboys abound. Blessed with such an abundance of inspiration, she only hopes that she can do them justice. Visit her website at www.vickilewisthompson.com.

Books by Vicki Lewis Thompson

HARLEQUIN BLAZE

*Sons of Chance

To get the inside scoop on Harlequin Blaze and its talented writers, be sure to check out blazeauthors.com.

All backlist available in ebook. Don't miss any of our special offers. Write to us at the following address for information on our newest releases.

Harlequin Reader Service
U.S.: 3010 Walden Ave., P.O. Box 1325, Buffalo, NY 14269
Canadian: P.O. Box 609, Fort Erie, Ont. L2A 5X3

To all the fabulous cooks I've known who have fed me terrific food that had the perfect mix of spices, wasn't either burned or raw, and never had bits of glass in it. I have committed all those sins and more, and suspect it may be time to hang up my potholders and abandon the field.

Prologue

AFTER FORTY-FIVE YEARS of marriage to Nelsie, Archie Chance knew timing was everything, especially when dealing with a touchy subject like food preparation. Nelsie was possessive about her kitchen, always had been. She'd rejected every suggestion to hire some help, but this time, Archie was determined to convince her.

He waited until they'd settled on the front porch for their usual after-dinner cup of coffee accompanied by a look-see at the mountains. Then he pretended his next move was an afterthought. "You know what? I'm gonna get that bottle of Bailey's and add a little to my coffee." Setting his mug on the small wooden table between their rockers, he stood.

Nelsie glanced up at him with a smile. "What are you plotting now, Archibald?"

He should have known she'd suspect him of having ulterior motives, but he pretended innocence. "Not a thing. I just like a little taste of Bailey's in my coffee now and again."

She didn't look convinced. "If you say so."

"Be right back." He walked inside and grabbed the bottle out of a cabinet he'd built years ago. From upstairs came the familiar sound of his son Jonathan and his daughter-in-law Diana having a row. Little Jack was crying, which any toddler would do if his parents yelled at each other like they had no sense.

Archie considered going up there and fetching Jack, but about that time the arguing stopped and Jonathan headed down the curved staircase holding his son.

"Taking Jack for a little ride." Jonathan avoided his father's gaze. "Won't be gone long."

"Okay." Archie watched Jonathan stride out of the house, his back rigid with anger. The marriage was not going well, but Archie wasn't surprised. Although Jonathan had made an effort because of the baby, he'd never been in love with that woman, and Diana wasn't easy to love, anyhow. Archie didn't know how to fix a problem like that.

So he decided to concentrate on the problem he *could* fix, or at least try to. Carrying the Bailey's, he walked back out to the porch, unscrewed the cap and held the bottle toward Nelsie. "Want some?"

"Think I will, after all." She held up her mug and he poured about a jigger's worth into it. She sighed heavily. "I hate it when they fight."

"Me, too." Archie doctored his coffee and put the cap back on before reclaiming his rocker. "But they're the ones who have to figure it out."

"I know. I just wish…"

She didn't have to finish the sentence for Archie to know what she wished—that Jonathan and Diana had been in love when they'd made that baby, so that getting married would have been a joy instead of an obligation. He took a sip of his coffee and was glad he'd added the Bailey's to soften the sharp edges of reality.

Pretty soon Jonathan came out of the barn leading Scout. He put Jack on first before mounting up and riding slowly across the meadow, holding Jack on the saddle in front of him. In spite of everything, Archie couldn't help smiling. That kid loved being on a horse as much as his daddy had at that age. Jonathan had tried teaching Diana to ride, but the effort had been doomed from the start.

"The mountains are pretty tonight," Nelsie said. "I love it when they get that pinkish glow."

"Yeah, it's nice." Gradually Archie's spirits began to lift, as they always did when he took time to appreciate his surroundings. The view from the porch was spectacular, and he could see it whenever he took the time. Besides that, he had a wife he cherished beyond belief, a devoted son, and the most amazing grandbaby in the world. All in all, he was one lucky SOB.

He'd finished about half his coffee when he decided to broach the kitchen-help idea. At least Nelsie had some Bailey's in her, which tended to mellow her out a bit.

"I can hear the wheels grinding over there," Nelsie said. "You might as well spit it out."

Archie looked over at her and grinned. She always could read him like a book. "All right. You've been against this in the past, but we're feeding quite a few cowhands at lunch these days, and—"

"Archie, you know I hate the idea of a stranger in my kitchen, not to mention the expense."

"But you're working yourself to a frazzle."

"If only Diana would—"

"Well, she's not going to, and we might as well accept the fact that she's not domestic." Archie hadn't figured out what Diana was good at besides shopping for clothes in Jackson.

She and Jonathan fought about her spending habits, but whenever Jonathan refused to give her money, she threatened to divorce him and take Jack. She would get that baby, too. Courts usually found in favor of the mother unless she was a drunk or a drug addict, and Diana was neither.

Archie peeked over at Nelsie to gauge her mood. He'd bet she was thinking about those shopping trips, too, judging from the way her mouth was set in a ruler-straight line.

But wishing for a different kind of daughter-in-law wouldn't get them anywhere. He pressed on. "I heard about someone who's looking for work. She came here from Nebraska with some guy who left her high and dry. She's been helping Edgar and Madge Perkins at the diner and they love her, but they can't give her enough hours because they already have a cook."

Nelsie turned to him. "Why doesn't she just go home to Nebraska?"

"Apparently she'd catch grief for her decision to leave in the first place. Besides that, she's become fond of our little town. Edgar and Madge said working for us would be the answer to her prayers."

Nelsie's expression softened. "So you've come up with a young woman who needs a helping hand."

He sensed victory. "It seems like we should at least try her out since we need a cook and she needs a job."

"You always did know how to get around me, Archibald Chance." She met his gaze. "I guess you'd better ask this girl to come out and talk with us. What's her name?"

"Her last name is Simms." Archie paused, trying to remember. "Her first name has two parts, like Mary Jane, or...no, wait, it's Mary Lou. Mary Lou Simms."

"Mary Lou Simms." Nelsie seemed to be trying out the name on her tongue. "You know, it might be nice to have another woman around the place."

Archie didn't miss the note of longing. Nelsie had dreamed of a daughter-in-law who was also a friend, but that hadn't happened. Maybe she'd find that female friend in Mary Lou Simms.

<u>1</u>

Present Day

FOOD WAS IMPORTANT to Matthew Tredway. He loved the taste, texture and smell of good food, and at six foot five and 220 pounds, he required a lot of it. But due to a series of air-travel snafus between Richmond, Virginia, and Jackson Hole, Wyoming, he hadn't had a decent meal all day.

Jeb Branford, a lanky, red-haired cowboy, had picked him up at the Jackson airport for the hour's drive to the Last Chance Ranch, where Matthew was scheduled to train a problem horse named Houdini. The potentially valuable stallion had never been ridden, let alone used as a stud. Matthew had been hired in a last-ditch effort to salvage the ranch's investment.

As a bonus, he looked forward to some down-home ranch cooking during the week or so he'd be at the Last Chance. Jeb had offered to stop somewhere for a bite to eat, but Matthew didn't want to look at another restaurant menu if he could help it.

"I'll just wait until we get to the ranch," Matthew

said. "I'm ready to kick back with a cold beer and some home-cooked eats."

"I really think we should stop somewhere." Jeb scanned the area as they headed out of Jackson. "About a mile down this road there's a burger joint that serves really—"

"No, thanks." A burger would do in a pinch, but Matthew longed for something that hadn't been part of an assembly-line operation. "I'm sure leftovers from the ranch kitchen will beat your burger joint, hands down."

"I wouldn't bet on it, Mr. Tredway."

"Matthew."

"Okay, Matthew, although it feels funny calling you that."

"Because I'm so old?" Matthew pegged the cowhand as early to mid twenties, and at that age, a thirty-five-year-old like Matthew probably seemed ancient.

"Heck, no!" The kid's blush nearly obliterated his freckles. "Because you're famous, Mr. Tred—I mean Matthew. You've been on TV and everything! I have your book, *Think Like a Horse,* and I've about worn it out. I lobbied for the chance to pick you up at the airport."

"Well, thank you." The concept of having fans always made him uncomfortable. Fame was a byproduct he hadn't counted on when he'd set out to do the work he loved. "I'm glad the book has been useful."

"Oh, definitely. Although we finally had to give up on Houdini, which is kind of cool since he's the reason you're here. I'm actually grateful to that horse for being a pain in the ass if he brought you here."

Matthew laughed. "I hadn't thought of it that way.

Ultimately, if my program is a success, I'll work myself out of a job."

"I doubt that will ever happen. There'll always be people who mess up a horse one way or another and need you to straighten things out. But listen, I really think you should eat before we get back to the ranch. We've passed up everything in Jackson, but Shoshone will be coming up in forty minutes or so. We could stop at the Spirits and Spurs or the Shoshone Diner."

"Why are you so dead set on feeding me before we get to the ranch?"

"Because the food there is terrible."

"Terrible? I find that hard to believe on a ranch the size of the Last Chance."

"It didn't used to be terrible. Mary Lou fixed great spreads." Jeb spoke in a worshipful tone. "Fried chicken with her special batter, amazing ribs, potato salad seasoned just right, stew with lip-smacking gravy, biscuits that would melt in your mouth…man, what I wouldn't give for some of that grub right now."

Matthew had a bad feeling about how this story would end. "Don't tell me Mary Lou up and died."

"No, not that bad. She got married."

"And left you high and dry?"

"For a little while, yeah. Mary Lou and Watkins, one of our top hands, are on a three-week honeymoon cruise, and nobody saw *that* coming because first of all she said she'd never marry him and second of all she's not much of a traveler. But the upshot is we're stuck with Aurelia Imogene Smith for the duration."

"That's quite a handle." Matthew pictured a sour-faced woman who insisted everyone address her with the whole blessed thing.

"Yeah, well, she told us that her mother gave her two fancy names to offset the boring last one. I don't know if those fancy names went to her head or what, but she claims to be a gourmet cook."

"Oh." Matthew smoothed a hand over his mouth to hide a smile. Most cowhands weren't big on gourmet vittles.

"The hands might be able to tough it out, but I feel especially sorry for the kids. Did anybody tell you about that program?"

"Yes, as a matter of fact. You've got, what, eight teenaged boys for the summer?"

"That's right. This philanthropist named Pete Beckett came up with the idea of using the ranch for a residential summer program for teenage boys. They've been labeled troublemakers, but I guess they like being on the ranch, because they haven't caused a single problem. I worry about this food thing, though. Teenagers need regular food. They don't want to complain, but I can see it in their faces that they don't like it."

"So what does she serve that's so bad?"

"Escargot." Jeb said it with a groan.

"Hmm. Pricey." Matthew wondered what sort of bills Aurelia Imogene was running up.

"It's snails, man! You don't eat something that crawls on the ground with slime coming out its ass! But she served a plate of those varmints and expected us to eat 'em. I don't *think* so."

"So you left them on the plate?" Matthew happened

to love escargots and hated to think of that delicacy going to waste.

"Hell, no. That would have been rude. We scooped 'em out of the shells like we planned to eat them. By now we know to bring plastic bags in our pockets when we come up to the main house for lunch, which is the only meal we eat there. Mornings and evenings we fend for ourselves down at the bunkhouse with stuff like canned chili. We always used to fill up at lunch. But now we're starving to death."

"What'd you do with the snails?"

"Gave 'em to the dogs."

Matthew winced at the travesty of that. Of course, maybe the snails weren't any good. Just because someone claimed to be a gourmet cook didn't mean they were.

"Some stuff's so bad even the dogs won't eat it."

Matthew was hardwired to solve problems, and this was one he had a stake in because he did love his food. "Can't you talk to somebody? Either her, or whoever hired her?"

"That's just it. She's Mary Lou's niece, and Mary Lou invited her to come and fill in. Nobody wants to offend Mary Lou because she's been good to us, and to be honest, I don't know what the Chance family thinks about the food because they've never said anything."

"So maybe they like it."

"I'd be surprised. I think they're just trying to ride it out like the rest of us. Plus, Aurelia's sweet as can be, and I'm sure she doesn't mean to make us gag. Nobody has the heart to hurt her feelings. In fact..." He glanced over at Matthew before sighing and turning his attention to the road again. "No, I can't do it. It's not fair to you."

"What's not fair?"

"One of the guys came up with the idea that you could pretend you were on a special diet or something, which she'd have to accommodate because you're an honored guest, and we'd all climb on board and say we'd eat the same thing to make life easier for her."

"I'm not going to lie to her about some bogus special diet."

"No, I don't think you should, either," Jeb said quickly. "I told the boys that. Bad idea."

"But I'd like to help. I've had some experience with fine dining, so maybe if I show that I appreciate what she's trying to do, I can make some subtle suggestions that would turn things around."

"Now that's more like it! But I still think we should stop for food before we get to the ranch."

Matthew shook his head. "That makes no sense. Before I can discuss food with her, I have to eat something she's made." He glanced at the clock on the truck's dashboard. They wouldn't arrive at the ranch until around seven, which was nine his time. By then he might not care what he ate.

"You're a brave man."

Matthew laughed. "That bad, huh?"

"I have two words for you. Goat cheese." Jeb made a face. "Find out if she's made something with goat cheese, and if she has, don't eat it. I guarantee you'll want to puke your guts out."

Matthew decided not to admit he was fond of goat cheese, too. Demand for his training skills now brought him offers from around the world. He'd learned to appreciate all sorts of food, assuming it was prepared well.

"So I should drop you at the main house?" Jeb asked.

"Right. I need to check in with Sarah Chance, anyway. If you'll take my duffel to the bunkhouse, you can put it on whatever bed you want me to use. I'll unpack after I've had something to eat."

"I hope you don't mind being down with us, but it's that or sleep in the main house with eight teenagers. I hear they're behaving themselves, but still."

"No worries. Bunkhouses are amongst my favorite places to sleep." Matthew gazed out at the majestic Tetons in the distance and the grassy meadows bordering the road. After spending the past few weeks in the manicured pastures of Virginia, he relished the rugged landscape of Jackson Hole especially on a warm July day. Born not far from here in Billings, Montana, he was a Westerner at heart.

At sixteen, he'd hired on at a working ranch outside Billings. There he'd discovered his gift for working with difficult horses when he'd befriended a mare that previously had trusted no one. His boss had been a talkative man, and soon Matthew had been in demand throughout the state.

When he'd transformed a Montana senator's unruly horse into a mount children could ride, he'd earned a national reputation for being a miracle worker. Many people had encouraged him to write a book about his methods, and that book had brought international attention to his training ability. He enjoyed the travel opportunities, but he welcomed a return to more familiar surroundings.

Jeb seemed happy about Matthew's fondness for bunkhouses. He glanced over with a smile. "We have a card game going most nights, in case you're interested."

"Deal me in. Once I assess the food situation, I'll be headed down there ready to play." He looked forward to spending a week at a place where Stetsons and hand-stitched boots were the norm. Jackson Hole felt a lot like coming home.

SPINACH SOUFFLÉ. Aurelia had spent the past hour sitting at the kitchen table going through her cookbooks in search of something spectacular for tomorrow's midday meal. The house was quiet for a change, because Pete Beckett had taken the teenagers to the Shoshone Diner to give Aurelia a break.

Aurelia appreciated the gesture. She enjoyed the kids, but they did make a racket, so the peaceful interlude was a good time to concentrate on her menu-planning. Going the soufflé route would be tricky with a crowd, but how gratifying if she could pull it off!

The big dining room sat thirty-two, but she wouldn't be feeding quite that many. The eight teens took up one of the round tables. The hands and whichever members of the Chance family showed up would occupy two more tables. She didn't have the baking dishes to make twenty-four individual soufflés, but since she didn't have an exact head count, several bigger ones everyone could share would work better, anyway.

Or maybe she should make ratatouille, instead. She leafed through another cookbook and found the recipe for that. She'd need eggplant, but she could run into town tomorrow and pick some up. Reading through the

list of ingredients, she lifted her thick hair off the back
of her neck to catch the evening breeze coming in the
kitchen window. The ranch didn't have air-conditioning
because it wasn't needed often in Jackson Hole, but they
could have used some AC today.

Aurelia's boss, Sarah Chance, had apologized for the
lack of cooling and had brought a fan into the kitchen
while Aurelia was fixing *brochettes aux rognons, de
foie et lardons* for lunch. Apparently this July had been
warmer than usual, although it didn't seem bad to Aurelia, who was used to Nebraska's summers.

This was her first trip out of Nebraska, and although
she was enjoying the chance to try recipes and cook
for a crowd, she couldn't imagine doing it on a regular
basis. She'd happily go back to her stress-free routine
of working at the bank and cooking for herself and her
friends on her days off.

As she puzzled over whether to serve the ratatouille
or the spinach soufflé the next day, she heard voices
coming from the hallway that led into the large dining room. One she recognized as Sarah's, but the deep
baritone didn't sound like any of Sarah's three adult
sons or Pete, who had recently become Sarah's fiancé.

As the voices drew closer and Aurelia heard Houdini's name mentioned, she figured out the horse trainer
had arrived. And he'd probably arrived hungry if Sarah
was bringing him back to the kitchen. Happy anticipation made Aurelia smile. She loved feeding people.

A moment later Sarah walked into the kitchen followed by a very tall man with shoulders a mile wide
and eyes bluer than the center of a gas flame. Aurelia
caught her breath as she stood to greet the most impos-

ing cowboy she'd seen since setting foot on the Last Chance. And that was saying something, because the ranch was chock-full of good-looking cowboys.

The horse trainer held his tan Stetson in one hand. He'd obviously been wearing it all day because his wavy brown hair bore the crease of it, along with a faint pink mark on his forehead, which she found endearing. His face and throat were bronzed by the sun, which presented a nice contrast to the blue denim Western shirt he wore. She didn't allow her gaze to travel lower in case he'd think she was giving him the once-over. She'd save that for when he wasn't looking right at her.

Aurelia's boss wasn't small at five foot nine, but this man made Sarah Chance look dainty. Sarah tucked her sleek bob, which she'd allowed to turn its natural white, behind her ears as she smiled at Aurelia. "Here's the magician who's going to solve our problems with Houdini. Matthew Tredway, may I present our cook, Aurelia Smith."

"Pleased to meet you." She held out her hand, which was engulfed by his much larger one.

His handshake was warm, and so was his smile. "Same here. I asked Sarah if you might have some leftovers for me. I haven't eaten much all day."

She'd seldom taken such an instant liking to someone, but Matthew had the square-jawed look of a man a girl could count on. "I'll be happy to fix you something." She couldn't seem to wipe the smile off her face, either. Her girlfriends had talked about instant sexual chemistry, but she'd thought they were imagining things because she'd never felt it before. In less than sixty seconds, Matthew Tredway had made a believer out of her.

Too bad she and Matthew were both only temporarily in the same place, but at least now she understood what her friends back home had been talking about. It really was like being struck by lightning, as evidenced by her pounding heart.

Before she'd fully processed her feelings, a commotion erupted in the main part of the house. Young male laughter and good-natured taunts, coupled with the sound of feet thumping on the stairs to the second floor, indicated the teenagers had returned from town.

Sarah glanced at Matthew and Aurelia. "If you two will excuse me, I'd better go check on the kids."

And Pete. Aurelia got such a kick out of watching the sixty-something couple. Anyone would think they were teenagers themselves as they held hands and shared a brief kiss now and then. Sarah had been widowed nearly three years ago, and her sons seemed happy that she'd found someone like Pete.

As Sarah headed out of the kitchen, Aurelia remembered her duties as the ranch cook. "Do you think the boys will want an evening snack? I have some roasted figs left."

Sarah turned back to her. "If I know Pete, he bought them all a slice of homemade pie at the diner, so I think they're set for the night. Thanks, though."

"Just wanted to make sure."

"I'd take some of those roasted figs," Matthew said.

Aurelia glanced at him. "Not until you've had a proper meal." When Matthew laughed, she realized how anal that had sounded. "Sorry, I've been dealing with teenagers for a week. If you want dessert first, you certainly can have it."

"That's okay." His smile creased his tanned cheeks. "I'll wait on the figs."

She had the insane urge to stand on tiptoe, clutch that smiling face, and plant one right on his gorgeous mouth. He was way too handsome for his own good.

But kissing him after knowing him for five minutes wasn't a great idea. Instead she walked over and clicked the oven knob before opening the industrial-sized refrigerator. "Then I'll warm up the leftover *brochettes aux rognons, de foie et lardons* we had for lunch."

"My French is pretty sparse, but I think I've had that before."

She turned, the foil-covered platter in her hand, and stared at him. "You have? I've never met anyone who's eaten it before."

"Tell me what's in it and I'll know for sure."

"Kidneys, liver and bacon on a skewer."

Matthew nodded. "That was my guess. Sounds great."

"Where did you have it?" Now she was nervous. Maybe the version he'd eaten had been better than what she'd fixed today.

"A restaurant on the Left Bank."

"In *Paris?*" Now she was *really* nervous.

"Yes. Ever been to France?"

"No. I'm not really into travel."

"You're not? Why?"

She shrugged. "I like the comforts of home too much, I guess. Traveling just doesn't appeal to me."

"But you could sample the food cooked by natives."

"I'd rather try making it at home myself." She wished she'd offered him something else, but too late for that now. Transferring several skewers to a baking dish, she flicked on the oven and slid the dish inside to heat. "But since I've never tasted the real thing like you have, my version may not be what you're used to."

"I'm sure it'll be terrific."

"I hope so. Reheated won't be quite the same as when they were first broiled." She gathered up her cookbooks so he'd have a place to eat. "Go ahead and sit." Then she had an inspiration. "Would you like some wine? It's not French, but Sarah always keeps some good California reds on hand."

"Only if you'll have a glass with me."

"Well…okay." She knew Sarah wouldn't mind. She'd have a little, to be hospitable. "Be right back." She opened the door to the walk-in pantry and ducked inside. Once there, she dithered over the wine selection, trying to imagine what a man who'd been to Paris would prefer.

"Want me to pick one?" Matthew walked into the pantry and the space instantly shrank.

"Um, sure. That makes sense." She stepped away from the wine rack, but there really wasn't anywhere to go. Once he moved in front of it, they were practically touching. The small space filled with his scent—a crisp, manly aroma that jacked up her pulse rate.

She became aware of his steady breathing as he pulled out a couple of bottles, checked the labels and moved on. She was afraid they weren't to his liking. "I know it's not a huge selection."

"No, it's great! I just don't want to drink up the pricey stuff!"

"But you should! Take the most expensive bottle!

From the way everyone's talked about you, they'd be honored for you to have it."

"I don't know what they've said, but the truth of the matter is that I'm an ordinary guy who can drink six-dollar wine and be perfectly happy. Here we go." He pulled out a bottle and showed it to her. "This will do fine."

She took a shaky breath and hoped he couldn't tell how his nearness affected her. "If you're sure."

"I am." He gestured toward the pantry door. "After you, mademoiselle."

Dear God, he even said it with a French accent. She brushed past him, aware of every point of contact with his solid body. She couldn't tell if he was attracted to her, too, but it really didn't matter.

He was here to train a horse and he'd spend his evenings at the bunkhouse, according to what Sarah had said. Tonight might be the only time she'd be alone with him for the rest of his stay. Considering they were from completely different worlds, that was probably for the best.

2

SHE WAS DYNAMITE, the ultimate definition of the word *hot*. Matthew wasn't sure what he'd expected when he'd walked into the kitchen to meet Aurelia Imogene Smith, but it certainly hadn't been a blonde with a drop-dead figure and eyes that sparkled like dew on spring leaves.

He understood immediately why nobody had criticized her food. Besides being great to look at, she was earnest about her job and achingly vulnerable in her need for validation. Telling her that most everyone hated her food would be mean.

He uncorked the wine and poured them each a glass.

"How about a salad?" she asked.

"Sounds good. Want help?"

"No, thanks. Go ahead and sit down. It'll only take a few minutes."

He took a seat at the table while she put together greens of various types with efficient motions that told him she was no novice in the kitchen. She didn't ask him the ranch-or-thousand-island question, either. Instead she mixed up some vinegar, olive oil and spices before tossing it with the greens.

So far he was inclined to think she was the real deal and the cowboys didn't have the kind of educated palate to appreciate her efforts. Still, he mentally crossed his fingers.

If the food was good, he'd have an easier task correcting the situation. If it was bad, he'd have to get creative. But that wasn't his only issue and probably not his biggest hurdle. Aurelia Imogene Smith turned him on.

His intense physical reaction to her defied logic. He'd dated a string of international beauties, skinny supermodels and jet-setters whose lifestyles mirrored his and who thought a man who trained horses was sexy. He didn't get that, although one girlfriend had taken great pains to explain that a man astride a horse evoked knights in armor and good guys in white hats, which appealed to women who craved romance.

Fortunately not all women who craved romance wanted permanence. Matthew had focused on a certain kind of woman—rootless, well-traveled, sophisticated and definitely tall because he liked that attribute. He was at the height of his career and had no intention of changing anything about his life.

Maybe someday, when he was tired of traveling or the offers stopped coming, he'd use the money he'd stashed away to buy a ranch and settle down. But until that time, he sought women who had the same rolling-stone philosophy as his own. Less chance of a broken heart that way.

Aurelia didn't fit the profile. He could tell from the way she'd reacted to his comment about Paris that she'd never been there. He'd be willing to bet she hadn't traveled much at all.

Her outfit—a white cotton peasant blouse over jeans and athletic shoes on her feet—suggested she wasn't particularly sophisticated, either. As for her height, he'd be amazed if she was much over five foot five. She was nothing like his usual girlfriends, and the total opposite of Elsa, the Swedish supermodel he'd broken up with a month ago.

And yet, from the moment he'd walked into the kitchen, he'd been assaulted by images of rolling naked with her on a mattress. The intensity of his reaction embarrassed him. He considered himself an evolved man who appreciated women for their minds as well as their bodies.

But if he were honest with himself, he didn't much care what was going on in Aurelia's mind. He just wanted to get his hands on her. That was unacceptable and he wouldn't follow through on the urge, but it was there, a humbling reminder that he wasn't quite as evolved as he liked to think.

Taking the baking dish from the oven, she transferred the meat from the skewers to a plate that already held a mound of salad. As she handed him the plate, he got a brief glimpse of cleavage. His johnson stirred, seeking Aurelia the way a divining rod seeks water. He ignored that unmannerly response and breathed in the aroma of the food, which smelled promising.

She pointed a finger at him. "Napkin. You need a napkin." Hurrying to one of the drawers in the array of oak cabinets, she pulled out a hunter-green cloth napkin and handed it to him.

"Thanks, but I can use paper."

"Not in this house. Sarah believes paper napkins

have eroded the elegance of the dining experience, not to mention cluttering up the landfill, so it's a rare occasion when she allows them."

"I respect that view." Matthew spread the napkin across his thighs. "This looks and smells delicious."

"Like I said, I'm not a trained chef. I just like to cook." She sat across from him, her expression anxious.

He raised his wineglass, which he hadn't touched because he'd been waiting for her to sit down. "Here's to your passion for cooking."

"I guess I can drink to that. It has brought me pleasure over the years." She touched the rim of her glass to his and took a sip of her wine.

He followed suit before setting the glass down and picking up his fork. He could feel her apprehension from across the table and knew that even if the food tasted like swill, he'd praise it to the skies.

It didn't taste like swill. Closing his eyes, he savored the first bite of gourmet food he'd eaten in some time. Then he looked at her. "This is awesome."

The tension went out of her shoulders and her smile lit up the room. "Really? You're not just saying that to be nice?"

"Hell, no. You have a gift, and I plan to enjoy it, so pardon me if I don't make conversation for a few minutes." He tucked back into the meal.

Her sigh was audible. "I'm so relieved. You know, I'm probably too sensitive, but I've had the feeling since I got here that not everyone loves my cooking. But, like I said, I'm probably imagining it."

No, you're not. But he said nothing. He had a mouthful of food, and besides, he hadn't quite decided on his approach.

"I did see one of the kids smuggling his lunch into a plastic bag once, and I heard another one saying something about the dogs."

"Mmm." He couldn't eat and talk, but he could eat and admire the way her shoulder-length blond hair caught the light from the lamp hanging over the kitchen table. That glorious hair would look terrific spread out on a pillow.

"I'll bet the boys think it's fun to give the ranch dogs a treat," she said. "We're not allowed to feed table scraps to Sarah's bassett hound because he's a couch potato. The other two, though, Butch and Sundance, get tons of exercise so a few handouts are okay. The kids are always playing with them."

Matthew was beginning to come up with a strategy. He took another bite, partly because he liked the food immensely and partly because he'd read somewhere that chewing helped a person think.

But he took a moment between mouthfuls to get in a comment. "It seems a shame for wonderful food like this to be given to a dog."

"They're kids, and disadvantaged kids at that. They don't know it's special."

"I'm not sure the cowboys do, either." He forked up another portion.

"Maybe not, although they seem appreciative that I'm cooking for them, and the food all disappears, so they must like it okay." She took a swallow of her wine.

He watched the movement of her lovely throat and imagined brushing it with his mouth, then nuzzling....

Hell. Just like that, he'd drifted from his charted course. He finished chewing and pulled his focus back to the problem. "If the ranch hands were better educated about food, they'd be raving."

"Would they? I thought cowboys were the strong, silent type."

"Not when it comes to food."

She gazed at him, her green eyes serious. "Are you saying they really don't like what I'm fixing?"

"I'm not saying that." And he wouldn't say it even if somebody shoved slivers under his fingernails. "I only have Jeb to go by, because he's the one I talked to on the drive from the airport, but since he didn't brag about the food here, I think it might be a little too sophisticated for his taste buds."

"Hmm." She took another sip of wine. "You could have a point."

"But maybe it's just Jeb." He returned his attention to his plate.

"I don't think so. Mary Lou left some recipes for me, but they were all so boring that I put them away. I know what you mean about the lack of enthusiasm from the cowboys, but I thought maybe they just didn't care that much about what they ate."

He thought of Jeb's rant about how much he missed Mary Lou's cooking. "I can understand why you'd get bored fixing the kind of food Mary Lou made. I'm guessing her recipes are for ordinary things like fried chicken, ribs, potato salad, stuff like that."

"Exactly! From what I could tell, she's been making the same kind of meals for years, and I thought everyone would like a change of pace."

"That's a good idea, but maybe it was too sharp a turn for them, considering they've probably never eaten gourmet food before."

She nodded. "I can see that might be a possibility."

"I have an idea for an experiment, if you'd like to hear it." And boy, did he like this idea. He hoped she would.

"Sure. Go ahead."

"I know plain food and I know gourmet food, so I could be your consultant and taste-tester while I'm here. We could look for recipes that are fun for you, but give a nod to the sort of food the cowboys are more used to. And then we could see what happens."

"That would be great, but I can't believe you have time to spare. You're here to work with Houdini, not help in the kitchen. I don't think Sarah or the Chance men would go for it."

He'd anticipated that argument. "I won't be training Houdini at night. After several hours of work, we'll need a break from each other."

"Yes, and you'll probably be exhausted."

He smiled. If she only knew how much the prospect of spending time with her would revitalize him. "I might be physically tired at the end of the day, but all we'd be doing is going over recipes and planning menus." He could imagine other activities, too, but he wouldn't count on it. She might not be the least bit interested in him.

"I'd want you to clear it with Sarah, and make sure she knows it wasn't something I asked for. They've been really good to me, and I don't want them to think I asked for extra help."

"I'll check with Sarah, but I really doubt she'll object." He had a hunch she'd be overjoyed if he stepped in and made some menu adjustments. Pete Beckett might have taken the kids to the diner tonight to stave off a revolt.

Aurelia gazed at him. "You're a very nice man, Matthew, to offer this when you probably should be relaxing down at the bunkhouse instead of coming up here to work."

He felt a pang of guilt. Although his original intent had been to help the cowhands out of a jam, now the plan was mostly an excuse to hang around Aurelia and get to know her better. He wasn't sure where that might lead, and he might be making a huge mistake.

She had home and hearth written all over her, and he couldn't offer her anything along those lines right now. But maybe, despite outward appearances, she wasn't looking for permanence. He'd never know unless he asked.

His plate was empty, and so was his wineglass. He should probably leave now. The boys in the bunkhouse expected him for a game of cards and he'd had a long day.

On the other hand, Aurelia had indicated a willingness to go along with his plan, and her cookbooks were still on the table. He glanced at them. "We could start tonight, if you want."

"Tonight? Oh, no. You must be jet-lagged. Besides, I've already narrowed it down to either spinach soufflés or ratatouille for tomorrow, so I'm okay for the time being. If Sarah agrees, we can start tomorrow night."

"I'm really not that tired." Adrenaline had kicked

in the moment he'd walked into the kitchen and caught sight of her. He hesitated. "Can I say something about your two options?"

She waved a hand. "Be my guest."

"I've had many spinach soufflés, and I'm sure with your talent you'd turn out something amazing. But I'd argue against making that for tomorrow."

"Why?"

"The color. To these guys, it'll look like you baked a frog."

She burst out laughing. "Okay, I can see you think like a cowboy. Apparently I don't because I never would have thought of that."

Her laughter charmed him. He was also impressed by her willingness to be flexible. "If you haven't been around cowboys before, I don't know how you could be expected to understand them."

"But I need to, obviously."

"That's where I come in."

"How about the ratatouille? I suppose that's out because of the name. I doubt cowboys are fond of rats."

"So don't call it that. Call it vegetable stew."

"And make it the authentic way?"

"Maybe not quite." He shoved back his chair and picked up his plate. "Let's have some more wine while we talk about how you can modify the recipe to make it more cowboy-friendly."

"I'll admit I'm intrigued." She stood, too. "Are you sure you're up to this?"

"I am if you are."

"Okay, then. That book on the top of the pile has the

ratatouille recipe in it. If you want to take a look, I'll
tidy up and bring out the baked figs."

"Great." Someone in his travels had told him that
figs were beneficial to a man's family jewels. Considering his state of mind, he couldn't think of a more ap-
propriate dessert for her to serve.

AURELIA COULDN'T TELL whether Matthew had offered
his services because he was a good guy or because he
found her attractive. A couple of times she'd noticed
what could be a gleam of interest in his eyes, but it
could also have been appreciation for her cooking. At
least he liked that about her.

She quickly refrigerated the remaining food and put
his plate in the commercial-sized dishwasher. When she
glanced at the table, he was intently studying the ratatouille recipe. "I can warm up the figs or serve them
cold with whipped cream. How would you like them?"

He glanced up. "Cold with whipped cream sounds
good."

"All right." When he focused those blue eyes on her,
she lost track of everything else.

She'd never licked whipped cream off a man's body,
but she wouldn't mind licking it off his. She could imagine popping open the snaps on that blue denim shirt and
squirting a trail of whipped cream down the middle of
his chest toward an even more interesting part of his
anatomy…oh, yeah. They could have fun times with a
can of whipped cream.

He glanced down at his shirt. "Did I spill food on
myself?"

Whoops. "No, no, I was just…wondering how you

stay so fit." *Way to go, girl. Now he knows for sure that you were ogling his chest.* Her cheeks grew hot. "I mean, it must be tough with all your traveling, and I know you love to eat, and…" Dear God, the more she explained, the worse it got.

Fortunately he looked more amused than offended. "The horses make sure I don't get lazy and fat."

"Well, that's logical." She struggled to remember what she'd been about to do that had started the whole whipped-cream fantasy. Oh, yes. Dessert.

"So go ahead and pile on the whipped cream. I'll work it off."

"Coming right up." She turned quickly back to the counter and resisted the urge to fan herself. She'd just bet he could work it off, in any number of ways. Right now she was picturing how many calories they could burn if they got naked.

Taking a deep breath, she uncovered the leftover figs. Darned if those figs didn't remind her of a certain part of the male anatomy. She hadn't planned to have any, but she found herself dishing a couple for herself.

Normally she would have whipped the cream herself instead of using a commercial version, but making her own would take too long. For the sake of convenience, she grabbed the pressurized can that had been in the refrigerator when she'd arrived last week.

After a few quick shakes, she pressed her finger against the nozzle. She hadn't used a can of whipped cream in years and she'd forgotten how much fun it was. She had to force herself to stop before she covered the figs completely.

Even then, she couldn't resist spraying some on her

finger and sucking it off before she put away the can. She had her finger in her mouth when she heard Matthew clear his throat. Turning, she met his gaze.

This time she had no doubt that the gleam in his eyes had nothing to do with her food and everything to do with her. Heat pooled low in her belly as his status changed from harmless crush to potential lover. Ah, but that was a bad idea, wasn't it? She hadn't been brought over from Nebraska to get horizontal with the horse trainer.

Perhaps he had the same thought, because he broke eye contact and looked down at the cookbook. "I think you should lose the eggplant." His voice was husky.

She was so focused on the undertone of lust that it took her a couple of seconds to register what he'd said and muster a protest. "Eggplant is the whole point to ratatouille." She returned the whipped cream to the refrigerator, pulled spoons out of the utensil drawer, and brought the two dishes of figs over to the table.

He cleared his throat again. "I realize that, but eggplant's a tricky vegetable when it comes to cowboys. They might accept it breaded and fried in eggplant parmesan, but I'm not sure they'll take to it in a stew."

"So ratatouille without the eggplant." She sat next to him because the idea had been to study the recipe together. "Maybe I should fix something else, instead." His warmth and his scent reached out to her.

"No, I think this will work." He pulled his dish of figs closer. "Thanks for fixing this."

"You're welcome." She cut through the whipped cream with her spoon and scooped up a bite of fig and cream. Sitting within easy touching distance of him made her tremble, and she took another calming breath. She didn't want to drop the mouthful of dessert in her lap.

But she was determined to eat and prove that she was in control of the situation. She put the spoon in her mouth, but not all the whipped cream made it. She had to lick away the excess.

She thought he hadn't noticed until she realized his breathing had changed. When she peeked over at him, he was watching her with that same intensity that played havoc with her pulse rate.

Closing his eyes, he pushed back from the table. "You know, maybe I should turn in, after all."

She had the distinct impression he was running away before he did something totally inappropriate. And how she wished he would. But he was acting like a responsible adult, so she would, too. "All right. But should I substitute something for the eggplant?"

"Yes." He picked up his bowl of figs. "I'll take these with me, if that's okay."

"That's fine. What should I substitute?"

"Potatoes." He headed out of the kitchen.

"Potatoes? Really?"

"Yes," he called over his shoulder. "Cowboys love potatoes. See you tomorrow, and thanks for a great meal!"

She stared after him, not sure whether to feel rejected by his abrupt departure or immensely complimented because he'd almost lost control of himself. She settled on feeling complimented.

But knowing they wanted each other this much changed everything. She wondered if he'd abandon the evening meal planning he'd suggested. If they went ahead with it, something was bound to happen. He had to know that as well as she did.

Would that be a mistake? From what she'd gathered from Aunt Mary Lou, the Chance family didn't interfere with their employees' personal lives as long as they fulfilled the duties they were hired for. Yet Aurelia didn't want to do anything that would reflect poorly on her aunt.

Being the aggressor in the relationship might look really bad, so no matter how much Matthew turned her on, she wouldn't pursue him. If he decided to resist temptation, then she would admire him from afar. But if he decided not to resist… Closing her eyes, she allowed herself to imagine the possibilities.

3

WOUND TIGHT FROM his encounter with Aurelia, Matthew carried his dessert down to the bunkhouse. He hoped the card game was still in progress. He desperately needed a distraction.

He'd been here less than an hour. Seducing the ranch cook within the first sixty minutes of arriving was not his style, but he'd come damned close to doing exactly that. He was the kind of man who liked to take it easy and work up to things. That was one of the qualities that made him a good horse trainer. So he needed to dial it back several notches.

Pushing open the screen door, he took in the welcome sight of six cowhands playing poker on a battered wooden table positioned in the middle of what was obviously the bunkhouse kitchen. They'd fortified themselves with beer, soda and various kinds of chips. A couple had cigars going. They all looked up from their cards as Matthew walked in.

"Hey, Matthew!" Jeb folded his hand and laid it on the table. "Let me introduce you to everybody." He pointed to a dark-haired cowboy on his left. "This joker is Tucker Rankin. He's only here for a couple of nights while his fiancée is at some forestry conference in Spokane, but the rest of these bozos live here full-time, so I'm afraid you're stuck with them and their snoring."

"Speak for yourself, carrot-top," a rugged blond guy said. "You're a damned buzz-saw."

"Am not, Shorty. That's coming from Danny's bunk."

"Hey!" A guy with prominent ears pointed his cigar at Jeb. "I do not snore. And that's a fact." He stood and extended his hand to Matthew. "Nice to meet you, Tredway. I'm Danny Lancaster. I admire your work."

"Thanks." Matthew transferred his dessert to his left hand so he could accept the handshakes of the rest of the poker players as they introduced themselves. Besides Shorty LaBeff and Danny Lancaster, the two cigar smokers, the table included Bob Gilbert, who wore wire-rimmed glasses, and Frank Delaney, who had a neatly trimmed mustache.

Danny glanced at Matthew's bowl of figs. "Those things look familiar. The trash is over yonder." He gestured with his thumb.

"Thanks, but I'm going to eat them."

"Don't put yourself through it. She'll never know the difference." Danny reached for the bowl. "Here, let me get rid of—"

"No!" Matthew jerked it back. "I want these! If the figs are half as good as the meal she fed me, they'll be great."

Danny stared at him, and then he broke into a wide grin that eventually turned to a chuckle and wound up as a belly laugh. Soon all the other cowhands were laughing, too.

"That's a good one, Tredway!" Danny clapped him on the back. "For a second there, I thought you were serious."

"He couldn't have been serious." Bob pulled out his shirttail and began polishing his glasses. "But it was good for a laugh."

"I am serious."

That set everyone off again.

"Yeah, right." Shorty grinned before sticking his cigar in the corner of his mouth. "Okay, joke's over. Pull up a chair, Tredway. Let's play some cards."

Matthew dragged a chair over and sat at the table. "I'm not kidding, guys. I enjoyed the meal Aurelia fed me."

Tucker, the guy who was only staying overnight, stared at him. "Then she must not have given you the lunch leftovers, because that stuff was awful."

"You can say that again." Frank picked up his cards. "What'd she call it?"

"Something French-sounding." Bob looked at his cards and put them face-down on the table. "Shetty fou lardy, or something like that. And I'm here to tell you it was definitely shetty."

"She gave me what you all had," Matthew said.

Frank wrinkled his nose, which made his mustache twitch. "Then you must possess different taste buds from the rest of us, because I don't know a single person besides you who liked it."

Matthew was walking a fine line if he wanted to avoid insulting these men, so he spoke with care. "I admit it was unusual, but as much traveling as I do,

I'm used to eating what's put in front of me. I guess it's possible that along the way my tastes have changed."

Jeb groaned. "And here I thought you'd be the perfect guy to fix the situation. But if you actually like her food, then you probably don't want her to change how she cooks."

"She doesn't have to change completely," Matthew said. "Just modify some. I already gave her a suggestion for tomorrow."

Everybody looked up from their cards.

"I don't suppose you suggested fried chicken and potato salad like Mary Lou makes." Shorty took a pull on his cigar and blew out the smoke. "I'm starting to have wet dreams about Mary Lou's cooking."

"I'm afraid it won't be fried chicken and potato salad, but I think you'll like it okay."

Jeb narrowed his eyes. "What is it?"

"It's a sort of vegetable stew."

Bob frowned. "No meat?"

"Hey," Tucker said, "don't be complaining about the lack of meat. She's liable to throw some kidneys in there left over from that shetty fou lardy."

"That wasn't meat," Bob said. "That was innards. I don't eat innards."

"And those things in the bowl you have there," Shorty added, "look like something a grown man should not be putting in his mouth, if you get my meaning."

Danny laughed. "Oh, you made your meaning clear all afternoon, Shorty. You want Tredway to take his dessert into the other room?"

"I just won't watch."

"They're perfectly good." Matthew dug into his dish

of figs, but couldn't resist needling Shorty a little before taking a bite. "Some folks say they keep you from being sterile."

Shorty puffed on his cigar. "My boys do just fine, thank you. Tucker, there, might want to eat some, seeing as how he's going to be a bridegroom in a few months."

"No, thanks," Tucker said. "I've made it this far without figs, so I think I'll take my chances."

"Suit yourselves." As Matthew had expected, the figs were great. He enjoyed them while the six men finished their current hand, and when they were done, so was he. He set the bowl on the floor by his chair. "Deal me in."

Frank shuffled. "Seven card stud." As he passed out the cards, he glanced over at Matthew. "Liked that dessert, did you?"

"Yep. Aurelia has skills in the kitchen. They just need to be channeled in a slightly different direction."

"I hope you can do it," Jeb said.

"I think I can." His big challenge would be slow-playing the sexual attraction between them. "All I ask is that you give tomorrow's lunch a fair chance. If you like it even a little bit, then you should probably tell her it's good. That'll make it easier for me to make other suggestions if this one goes over."

"Could she maybe bake some corn bread to go with it?" Tucker asked. "You can put up with a so-so meal if you have a good hunk of corn bread."

"I'll see what she says." He'd have to find an opportunity to talk with her in the morning in order to make that request. The thought jacked up his heart rate. "But she can't know that we've discussed all this."

"Right," Jeb said. "Matthew is like our go-between, but we have to make sure Aurelia doesn't figure that out."

Danny clamped down on his cigar as he fanned out his cards. "He's like a hostage negotiator, and we're the hostages." He threw a chip in the middle of the table. "Ante up, suckers. I've got me a powerhouse here."

As the poker game progressed, Matthew lost more than he won, which wasn't surprising. His thoughts kept drifting back to Aurelia Imogene Smith, which didn't make for good poker-playing. The cowhands chalked it up to jet-lag, and he willingly agreed.

If he and Aurelia became lovers, and he thought it was likely they would eventually, he'd rather not have the whole ranch know about it. However, he wasn't sure if he could avoid that. His comings and goings from the bunkhouse would be noted.

No matter what, he couldn't let his interest in Aurelia overshadow his purpose in being here. While a new hand was being dealt, he brought up the subject of Houdini. "Any tips on the horse I'm here to train before I get started tomorrow?"

Jeb laughed. "Tucker, anything you want to say on the subject of Houdini?"

"Yeah. He's a pain-in-the-ass, but I love that horse. If it hadn't been for him escaping on Christmas Eve, I might never have met Lacey, the love of my life."

Matthew glanced at him. "That sounds like a good story."

"Don't get him started," Danny said. "The boy's got it bad."

"Lacey's a nice girl." Bob picked up his cards and adjusted his glasses. "Probably too good for you, Tuck, but she seems as blinded by love as you are."

"Thanks for that vote of confidence, Bob." Tucker fanned his cards. "The point is, Matthew, that Houdini's gift for opening stall doors and escaping every chance he gets turned out good for me because I chased him over to the cabin where Lacey was staying, which led to us getting together. But the horse is too smart for his own good. He'll keep you on your toes."

Matthew consulted his cards. "I'd rather have him be smart than dumb as a box of rocks. A smart horse can be trained."

"In theory, that's true." Danny chewed on his cigar. "But we have some fine horse trainers on this ranch, including those at this table, and we haven't made a dent in that horse's behavior. If he had a middle finger, he'd be giving us the Italian salute."

"That's okay. I like a challenge."

Shorty glanced across the table at him. "If you can fix Houdini and our food problem, then drinks are on me at the Spirits and Spurs before you leave."

"Whoa." Danny reared back in his chair. "That's big medicine, there, Shorty. I can't remember the last time you bought a round of drinks."

"Bite me, Lancaster."

Matthew grinned. It was good to be back in the bunkhouse of a working ranch. Add in an excellent ranch cook who looked like Aurelia, and he couldn't think of anywhere he'd rather be, at least for the next couple of weeks.

ALTHOUGH AURELIA WOULD have happily fixed breakfast for Sarah every morning, Sarah insisted on making breakfast for both of them each day. Sarah was a good cook, though not particularly imaginative. Aurelia didn't mind since the shared meals gave her a chance to know the woman who had been Aunt Mary Lou's employer and friend all these years.

While Sarah scrambled eggs, fried bacon and toasted bread, Aurelia sat at the table with her coffee and the ratatouille recipe.

"You and Matthew must have bonded over the subject of gourmet cooking last night." Sarah glanced over her shoulder at Aurelia.

That wasn't all they'd bonded over, but Aurelia wasn't about to mention the sizzling chemistry between them. "Have you talked to him?" After a week, she still wasn't used to the ungodly hour everyone got out of bed on a working ranch.

"He called an hour ago, before he headed down to the barn to get started with Houdini. He praised your cooking to the skies."

That got Aurelia's heart pumping. "That's nice to hear, since he's eaten in restaurants all over the world, including Paris, the food capital of the world."

"I know." Sarah turned off the stove and pulled two plates from the cupboard. "He's an interesting combination of down-home cowboy and jet-setter."

And gorgeous, super-sexy, male. "I was a little worried that my *brochettes aux rognons, de foie et lardons* wouldn't be up to his standards, but he liked it."

"He told me he did." Sarah filled their plates and

brought them over to the table. "He also said that he'd get a kick out of consulting with you on future menus."

"Did he?" Aurelia did her best to act mildly interested while her heart thumped so fast she worried that Sarah would hear it. If he'd mentioned that possibility to Sarah, then the menu-planning sessions were still on. And if the menu-planning sessions were still on, then so was the possibility that they'd become lovers.

But she didn't want Sarah to suspect any of that. "How do you feel about Matthew helping me with my job?" she said as casually as possible.

"Whatever he wants works for me." Sarah sat down and spread her napkin in her lap. "It was a coup getting him here in the first place. He's in demand all over the world, and we're fortunate he took us up on our offer."

Aurelia had figured out that Matthew was a rock star among horse people. If she thought for even one second that Matthew was the sort of man who took advantage of his position to get women, her infatuation with him would end.

But he wasn't like that. When the heat between them had threatened to consume them both, he'd left, because it was too soon, too fast. Obviously from his actions, he'd proved that he had standards and scruples. That made him even more irresistible to her.

Sarah buttered her toast. "The more relevant question is, what do you think of the idea? For the time you're at the Last Chance, this is your kitchen, and you may not want some six-foot-five cowboy invading your space and making suggestions."

Oh, but she did. And the suggestions could range far beyond the subject of food preparation. She wasn't an idiot, though. Whatever they shared would be brief, an interlude in both of their lives that would never be more than a memory to savor. But she wanted that memory.

Until she'd accepted Mary Lou's offer, she'd never left Nebraska. Her family didn't travel, and Mary Lou was the only relative who lived more than a hundred miles away from Aurelia's home town. Her aunt's honeymoon cruise, which included a trip through the Panama Canal, was unimaginable and frightening to the rest of the family.

Aurelia had inherited that same reluctance to travel, so the trip to Jackson Hole might be the biggest adventure she'd have in her entire life. Matthew Tredway might be as close to a rock star as she'd ever get. If he wanted to invade her kitchen—or her bedroom—then she would fling open the door and let him in.

None of that, however, would be part of her answer to Sarah. "If getting involved with the menus interests him, then it's fine with me," she said. "With his background, I trust him to give good advice."

"Great. That's settled, then. As he mentioned to me, he won't be training Houdini at night, so that would be a good time to come up to the house and consult with you about the food for the next day."

"That's fine." More than fine. They'd have the kitchen to themselves.

Sarah gazed at Aurelia over the rim of her coffee cup. "I want to make sure you don't have a problem with Matthew doing this. I promised Mary Lou I'd watch out for you, so if this makes you uncomfortable, tell me and I'll shut him down. I want to make him happy, but not at the expense of my staff's morale."

And that, Aurelia thought, was why Aunt Mary Lou idolized Sarah Chance. She was loyal to those she'd committed to, and even a big-deal horse trainer celebrity didn't take precedence over the welfare of her staff, including someone like Aurelia, who would be here such a short time.

Sarah couldn't know that Aurelia lusted after Matthew Tredway. If Aurelia had her way, Sarah would never know, but that was probably unrealistic. Even though Aurelia had been on the ranch a relatively short time, she'd figured out that Sarah was tuned in to almost every aspect of ranch life. Hardly anything got past her.

Right now, Sarah was waiting for an answer to her question. Would Aurelia object to having Matthew, aka muscular hero, show up every evening to discuss the next day's menu? Hardly. But she didn't want to appear too eager, either.

"Let's try it for a night or two and see how it goes," Aurelia said. "If it's not working out, I'll let you know."

"Perfect." Sarah tackled her breakfast in earnest. "My main concern is Houdini, of course. I hope Matthew's able to turn that horse around. If it relaxes him to think about food and menus every evening, so much the better. But he's here to train Houdini, and that's the primary goal. Houdini's a valuable stud, and we're not getting the income out of him that we need to. We also hope to train him as a cutting horse eventually. Matthew's supposed to make him a joy to deal with."

"I'm sure he will." What Aurelia knew about training horses could fit on the head of a pin, but she could feel Sarah's frustration with a horse that wasn't earning his keep. Matthew had been hired to cure what ailed Houdini, and as the new kid on the block, Aurelia wasn't about to mess with that.

4

A COUPLE OF HOURS LATER, as Aurelia had begun gathering her ingredients and spices for the ratatouille, Matthew appeared in the kitchen. He was a very different Matthew from the one she'd seen the night before. This one wore an old T-shirt that was splotched with sweat and dirt, a T-shirt that strained at the seams over spectacular biceps, pecs and deltoids.

Yesterday's shirt had somewhat disguised his physique, but this one left nothing to the imagination. He'd been wearing his hat when he'd come through the door, but he took it off to reveal hair that had a tendency to curl when he was hot and sweaty. Two damp tendrils lay across his forehead.

Caught up in the glory that was Matthew, she could barely remember her name. But she sure as hell remembered his, and imagined the joy with which she'd call that name in the midst of a spectacular orgasm. It was quite a vivid picture for ten-thirty in the morning.

"I could use some carrots," he said, seeming distracted. "Or if you don't have those, apples will work."

"I have both, and good morning to you, too."

His smile was sheepish. "Sorry. When I'm working, I have a bad habit of getting tunnel vision. And speaking of that, there was something else I wanted to ask you about. What was it?" Frowning, he gazed at the floor and tapped his hat against his denim-covered thigh. His jeans were more worn and formfitting than the ones he'd had on the night before, too.

"Did you want to discuss what time you'll be coming to the house tonight?"

He glanced up, his gaze now focused and intent. "Sarah talked to you about that?"

"Yes." She couldn't stop looking at him. She wanted to walk over, peel the shirt from his body and lick the sweat from his powerful chest. Who needed whipped cream with a guy like Matthew?

"You're okay with that plan?"

"Why wouldn't I be?"

He held her gaze for a long, hot moment. "Just checking."

Her toes curled inside her running shoes. She knew exactly what he was checking. He wanted to find out if she'd had a change of heart following their mutual admiration society the night before. He wanted to know whether she was willing to see where this sexual chemistry might lead them.

"I think it's a fine idea," she said, in case he had any doubts about her feelings. "I'm ready for whatever suggestions you want to make." That was a little bolder in the double-meaning department than she'd intended, but she let the statement stand.

The effect on him was instantaneous. A flame leaped in his blue eyes and he took an involuntary step forward. Then he paused as if he'd belatedly realized this wasn't the time or the place.

He nodded. "Good. I'm glad."

"Do you want the carrots and apples cut up or whole?"

He blinked as if he had no clue what she was talking about. Then the fog cleared. "Cut up, if you don't mind. And if you could put them in a plastic bag, that would be great."

"Sure thing." She pulled the carrots out of the refrigerator and took a couple of apples from a bowl on the counter.

"Or I can cut them up," he said. "I'm sure you're busy getting lunch ready."

"That's okay." She got out a cutting board and set to work. "I'm the cook, which probably extends to making treats for the horses. This is for Houdini, right?"

"It is."

"How's everything going with him?"

"If we can stay on schedule, I'll ride him around the corral this afternoon."

She turned to him, knife poised in midair. "Ride him already? Sarah told me he's never been ridden."

"Well, today's the day."

His quiet confidence registered on her lust-o-meter. So would his competence if he pulled this off. She continued slicing up the apples and carrots. "You should probably sell tickets."

"I doubt anybody would buy them."

"I would."

"Then I hereby offer you a complimentary ticket

to the official riding demonstration featuring Houdini and yours truly."

"How will I know when it is?"

"You might want to come out around four. I'm shooting for that."

She scooped the pieces of carrot and apple into a plastic bag, zipped it closed and walked over so she could hand it to him. "It's only the first day. I'm sure nobody expects you to ride him on the first day."

"But I do."

She admired his attitude even more than she admired his body, and that was saying a lot. "Understood."

"Thanks for the horse treats." His hand brushed hers as he took the bag.

"Anytime." And she meant that sincerely. If Matthew would consider walking in here once or twice a day in a tight T-shirt, he'd contribute substantially to her job satisfaction.

His gaze lingered on her face, touching her hair, her eyes, her mouth. For one brief moment it dropped to her cleavage before moving back to her eyes. "See you at lunch."

She could barely breathe. "Right."

"I need to go." But he didn't move.

"Yes." Heat sluiced through her, and if he didn't leave soon, she was liable to forget her vow not to be the aggressor in this relationship.

"What time tonight?"

A slight roughness in his voice told her that he was anticipating it as much as she was. "How about eight?"

"I'll be here."

"Me, too." And she'd take a second shower and put on her sexiest underwear before then.

His expression softened, almost as if he might kiss her, but then he shook his head and turned. "Gotta go." Putting on his hat, he walked away with a determined stride. But at the kitchen doorway, he stopped abruptly.

When he turned, she held her breath, certain he was about to close the distance and take her in his arms, after all. Heart beating wildly, she moistened her lips. "Did you forget something?"

"Yes." But instead of coming back and scooping her into a scorching embrace, he stayed by the door. "What do you think of baking some corn bread to go with the ratatouille?"

She almost laughed. She'd been thinking passion and he'd been thinking corn bread. There was no predicting what was going through a man's mind. "I could do that."

"Great. See you later." And he was gone.

Turning back to the counter, she took a deep breath. The guy was seriously potent, and she'd have to stay focused on her cooking this morning or no telling what she'd end up serving for lunch. She opened the spice drawer looking for the jar of bay leaves.

She'd just located it when she was startled by the sound of booted feet and a strong hand gripping her arm. Matthew spun her around, pulled her against his chest and kissed her. She barely had time to register the heat of his body and the firm pressure of his sculpted mouth before he let her go.

His breathing was ragged as he stepped back and crammed his hat on his head again. "Some things can't be put off," he said. "And that was one of them." He turned and left the kitchen.

She tingled from head to toe and blood rushed in her ears. For several seconds she stood clutching the jar of bay leaves, her gaze unfocused as she relived the thrill of being accosted by the likes of Matthew Tredway. A delicious shiver went up her spine as she recalled the imprint of his body on hers and the hunger in that one fierce embrace.

He'd been in total command of the moment, sure of himself and what he intended to do. If he could pack that much into one quick kiss, she had a lot to look forward to tonight.

As MATTHEW RETURNED to the corral and Houdini, the taste of Aurelia's mouth was on his lips and her scent clung to his clothes. He'd briefly satisfied the craving growing within him, and like a light snack before a meal, it would have to do.

When he'd first walked into the kitchen, his mind had been occupied with the challenge of training Houdini. He'd thought his concentration would hold long enough to get some carrots, ask about the corn bread and leave before succumbing to Aurelia's appeal. He'd miscalculated. Within a very short time, lust had claimed every brain cell and body part.

Although seducing her this morning was out of the question, his libido had demanded some sort of satisfaction. He'd tried to deny that urge and had nearly made it out of the house. Apparently his willpower was no match for the temptation of Aurelia's mouth, though, and he'd turned around.

If he'd ever felt this kind of desperate need for a particular woman, he couldn't recall it. During the night, as he'd lain in his narrow bunk listening to the cowhands snore, he'd searched for an explanation as to why Aurelia affected him this way.

Sometime in the early-morning hours he'd come up with the answer. After years of dating women who were rolling stones like he was, he'd developed an itch for a hearth-and-home kind of woman. Aurelia, with her cooking skills and voluptuous body, could give him that.

With luck, once he'd scratched this particular itch, he'd be fine again. He certainly hoped so, because he had no intention of giving up his career, and travel was a built-in requirement. Plus he liked to travel and had no real desire to stay in one spot and become domesticated.

Tonight he'd say all that to Aurelia, because he didn't want her going into this with any illusions about permanence. He doubted she had those thoughts. She'd already stated that travel wasn't her thing.

He figured that when the right guy came along, she'd get married and have kids. Any woman taking a good look at Matthew's life would see that he wasn't the type to settle down and raise a family. But it wouldn't hurt to make sure Aurelia understood that.

Houdini watched him walk toward the corral. Matthew took out a slice of apple and began eating it. With animals as with people, sharing food could be a bonding thing. Matthew was working on building trust.

Fortunately the horse accepted a bridle, or the task would be even harder. Matthew had started out the day by leaning all over Houdini, getting him used to having an arm draped over his back. Finally he'd eased a saddle blanket on and Houdini hadn't pitched a fit.

Normally a saddle would be the next step, but Houdini had a real fear of them, according to Emmett Sterling, the foreman. Apparently the former owners had mentioned an incident where they'd managed to put a saddle on him but hadn't cinched it tight before Houdini started bucking. The saddle rotated around to his belly and Houdini had panicked.

A saddle wasn't necessary in order for Matthew to ride him today. Just the blanket would work, especially if Matthew had created the bond he wanted. To that end he'd also spent time playing with the horse and grooming him.

Although Matthew was hot and sweaty from the morning's work, Houdini looked spectacular. His black and white coat gleamed and his long white tail was completely free of tangles and burrs. For Matthew, the training process wasn't a battle of wills. Instead it was an exercise in mutual respect and cooperation between human and horse.

His method took enormous amounts of patience, and often ranch owners like the Chance men didn't have the time to be that patient with a horse that had been spoiled as a colt the way Houdini had. The people who had originally bought him had intended to train him, but they'd botched what little they'd done and had eventually left Houdini to train himself.

He'd done it, too, Matthew thought with a smile as he opened the gate and walked into the corral. He'd trained himself to be so independent that he had no intention of carrying a human on his back. When he was bored, he unfastened the latch on his stall and took a stroll around the barn, sometimes letting the other horses out, too, if he felt like it.

Houdini walked toward Matthew, who held an apple slice in his outstretched hand as he whistled softly.

"You're not a bad guy," Matthew said as the horse took the piece of apple and stood munching it, his tail swishing flies. Matthew stroked Houdini's silky neck and scratched beneath his mane. "You've just been allowed to get away with murder."

Houdini nuzzled Matthew's pocket for more treats.

"Later. We have work to do first."

A young male voice still finding its range called over from the fence. "You going to ride him today, Mr. Tredway?"

Matthew glanced over at the short, wiry boy leaning on the rail. "That's the plan, Lester." Matthew had met all eight of the teenagers earlier while they'd been busy mucking out the stalls. He remembered Lester because he was smaller than the rest and didn't seem to be totally accepted by the other boys. Yet Emmett had told Matthew privately that Lester could clean two stalls in the time it took any of the others to clean one. He seemed to love the work, but the other boys had accused him of trying to suck up by working so hard.

"Will it be like a rodeo?"

"I hope not." Gazing at Lester, Matthew hatched a plan. "Are you busy right now?"

"Nope. Finished what I had to do so I could watch you with Houdini."

"Want to help me?"

"You bet!" He started to clamor over the fence.

"Wait a sec. Go get your riding helmet first."

Lester's dark eyes widened. "You're gonna put me up on him?"

"I'm thinking about it. You're lighter than I am, so you could ease him into the idea." Matthew would keep a firm hold on the horse and Lester could jump off if things got dicey. "That's if you want to."

"Are you kidding? Of *course* I want to. Be right back." He took off at a run.

"Okay, Houdini." Matthew rubbed the stallion's nose. "I'm taking a chance on you, so don't let me down."

Lester came back in a flash, buckling his riding helmet as he sprinted toward the corral.

"Slow down," Matthew called as softly as he could and still be heard. "No rapid movements and no loud noises."

"Oh." Lester downgraded to a walk. "Sorry."

It had occurred to Matthew this morning that the teenagers spending their first summer on a ranch weren't much different in temperament from Houdini. Most of them had gotten into trouble due to lack of structure, just like the horse.

So after Lester climbed into the corral, Matthew explained Houdini's issues while Lester fed the horse a few pieces of carrot. Lester nodded as if he completely understood. Matthew supposed he did.

"Now just start loving on him," Matthew said. "Get him used to how you smell. Talk to him, too. In other words, treat him like a friend."

Stepping back, Matthew allowed Lester to move in. The boy began by stroking the horse and telling him how awesome he was. Then Lester proceeded to lay all his sins at Houdini's feet. He confessed how much trouble he'd caused himself and others by doing things he shouldn't, and he urged the horse to go straight or face the consequences.

Matthew bit his lip to keep from laughing. But as Lester continued his earnest conversation by giving examples of friends who'd also nearly ruined their lives, Matthew looked on in amazement.

The horse couldn't understand the words, but something was going on between those two, some level of communication that even Matthew, with all his years of experience, hadn't achieved. Houdini lowered his head so that Lester could scratch it better, and bumped his nose playfully against the boy's knee during the long monologue.

With a huge smile on his face, Lester glanced over at Matthew. "He likes me."

"He sure does." Matthew wondered if Houdini's former owners had had a teenager who'd spent time with the horse. That would partially explain Houdini's reaction, but Matthew thought it went deeper than that. Lester and Houdini just seemed to get each other. It reminded him of a scene out of *The Black Stallion*.

As the boy and horse continued their love fest, Matthew decided the time had come to try his experiment. "Why don't you ask him if he'll let you up on his back?"

"Okay." Lester rubbed Houdini's nose. "Houdini, how about giving me a ride, buddy? I'm just a kid, and I only weigh ninety-one and a half pounds, so you'll barely feel me. Plus I'll get street cred like you wouldn't believe. So can I?"

Houdini snorted.

Lester glanced over his shoulder at Matthew. "I think that means yes."

"All right. Here's the plan. I'll help you on but we'll go slow, and I'm going to hang on to Houdini in case you have to get off in a hurry."

"I won't have to." Lester's smile was filled with confidence. "Houdini likes me. He won't buck me off, will you, boy?"

Houdini butted Lester's chest.

Lester laughed. "But I think we should give him one more piece of carrot to chew on, so he'll have something else to think about while I climb up there."

"You have the instincts of a horse trainer, Lester."

"That's because I'm gonna be one, like you."

Matthew was impressed with the conviction in Lester's voice. "When did you decide that?"

"About ten minutes ago."

Now that was humbling. So far as he knew, Matthew had never changed the course of a person's life, but he had a hunch that he'd just changed Lester's. "It's a great life," he said, and was surprised at the emotion clogging his throat. He hadn't realized that being idolized by a young boy could affect him so much. "So, ready to mount up?"

"Yep."

"Okay, I want you to climb up on the fence and I'll bring him over to you. That way you can ease onto him gradually."

"Okay."

Once Lester was on the fence, Matthew led Houdini over. "Keep your left hand on the fence as you slide your right leg over. And talk to him. Talking's good."

Assuring the horse that everything would be just fine, Lester put one leg over his back and slowly began to transfer his weight. Houdini shivered but stayed where he was.

"Now take hold of his mane with your right hand."

Houdini swung his head around to see what was going on, but other than that, he didn't react. So far, so good.

"Grab his mane with your other hand and shift all your weight onto him. That's it. Sink your weight into your heels and lower your center of gravity. Good. Sit up straight and tall. Excellent." Matthew gripped the reins in anticipation of an explosion.

Amazingly, it never came. Houdini shifted his weight and looked back to see if Lester was still up there. Apparently the horse was fine with that. Matthew let out a breath and relaxed his hold on the reins.

Lester made a little clicking noise with his tongue.

"Hey, don't—" But Matthew had no more time to protest because Houdini started off at a slow walk, and Matthew followed along, holding the reins.

"See that?" Lester said. "He's letting me ride him."

"Yes." Matthew mentally crossed his fingers that this little stunt wouldn't backfire. "So he is."

They made a circuit of the corral, which was about all Matthew's nerves could take. "I'm going to guide him over toward the fence again," he said. "When I pull back on the reins, you say *whoa*. Then I want you to climb off the same way you got on."

"Aw." Lester frowned at Matthew. "Can't we keep going?"

"Better to make it short the first time and teach him to stop on command. Okay, tell him to whoa."

Lester did as he was told and Houdini came to a halt as if he'd suddenly become a perfectly trained horse. Matthew knew better, and he was immensely relieved when Lester was back on the fence.

"I rode him." Lester's frown gave way to a look of pride. "I was the first person to ride that horse."

"Yes, you were. If you want, I'll talk to Emmett about giving you time this afternoon to try it again."

"That would be great!"

"And if we can keep this on the down-low, you might be the one putting on a demonstration later instead of me."

"Wow." Lester's eyes shone. "That would be amazing. I won't say anything to anybody, I promise!"

"Good." Matthew stroked Houdini's silky neck. "Because it's about time to go in for lunch, and it might be hard to keep that secret."

"Nope. I can do it. But I wouldn't mind skipping lunch. I *hate* the lunches here."

"I have a feeling today's might be better."

"Boy, I hope so. Yesterday's was disgusting."

Poor Aurelia, Matthew thought as he and Lester walked Houdini back to the barn. She tried so hard, and her efforts were wasted because this wasn't a sophisticated crowd.

They really would need to do a little menu-planning tonight. But he hoped it wouldn't take long, because he had some other activities in mind.

5

AURELIA HAD HER misgivings about the meal she served for lunch. Substituting potatoes for eggplant in ratatouille seemed like a sacrilege, but she'd made the adjustment and also allowances for the varying cooking times of potatoes and eggplant. She had no recipe for corn bread other than Mary Lou's, which was uninteresting, but she didn't have time to get creative with the ingredients.

Matthew gave her a warm smile that jacked up her pulse rate as she put his plate in front of him. "Looks like a great vegetable stew," he said.

That reminded her that she wasn't supposed to mention the French name, although in all good conscience she couldn't call it ratatouille without the eggplant. "I hope you like it."

"Corn bread smells good," said Bob Gilbert, one of the few cowboys she knew who wore glasses.

"Thank you." She gave him his plate. "It's Mary Lou's recipe." Maybe she imagined it, but she could swear someone let out a heartfelt sigh. She was beginning to think Matthew was right, and cowboys were vocal when they liked the food, but not so much when they didn't.

She continued to get the food on the table along with help from Sarah, who'd recently begun pitching in to serve and clear the lunch meal. It gave her a chance to interact with each of the cowhands and underscored her position as the matriarchal head of the family. Aurelia was constantly impressed by the ways in which the Chance family kept the ranch functioning as a loyal unit.

As she moved back and forth between the kitchen and the dining room, she thought about Western movies she'd watched in which the cowboys ate whatever came from the chuck wagon, because if they complained, they'd get nothing. Apparently cowboys were both loyal and stoic. If she was the replacement cook, they'd put up with her, even if she'd been badly missing the mark with their meals.

Well, then, she'd be more open to whatever suggestions Matthew made tonight. But as she glanced across the room at him, she thought about what he might suggest that had nothing to do with food, and she retreated to the kitchen before someone noticed that she was blushing for no good reason.

Because she'd been so involved with converting the ratatouille to a potato-based dish, she hadn't had a chance to come up with a creative dessert, either. At the last minute she'd fallen back on another of Mary Lou's recipes, double chocolate chip brownies.

She brought those out after she and Sarah had cleared the lunch dishes, and she heard a distinct murmur of approval running through the room like a soft breeze.

After she'd delivered a plate of brownies to each table, she walked over to Matthew's seat, grabbed his water glass and a spoon, and tapped it to get everyone's attention.

Matthew glanced up at her, his eyebrows raised.

She gave him a quick smile and returned to the audience she'd created with the spoon-and-water glass routine. "It's been brought to my attention that some of you might not be totally happy with the meals I've served."

At first everyone looked guilty, but then a chorus of protests arose, assuring her that her cooking was great, and they appreciated all her efforts, yada, yada, yada. The comments came mainly from the tables dedicated to the cowhands and the teenagers. The Chance family seemed to be observing the proceedings with interest, but they didn't take sides.

Aurelia cut off the protestations by tapping on the glass again. "You're all sweethearts for trying to make me feel better, but I got the message from the way everyone reacted to Mary Lou's corn bread and her double chocolate chip brownies."

"Well, we do like those brownies," said Shorty LaBeff. "You'd have to be dead not to go for those."

Heads nodded all around the dining room.

Aurelia took a deep breath. "I can see why the brownies are a favorite. Chocolate is a mood elevator."

Danny Lancaster, the cowboy with very big ears, raised a hand. "And I vote we ride that elevator to the top! More chocolate!"

That got a laugh, but Aurelia tapped her spoon again because she was determined to have her say. "Mary Lou is a wonderful cook, and I don't blame you for being partial to her recipes. But since you're stuck with me for another two weeks, that gives you a chance to try some different foods, and personally, I think that's always a good thing."

That seemed to be a new concept, because quite a few of the men looked at her in bewilderment. That made her even more determined to open their minds to unusual dishes. "I propose a compromise. I'll continue to provide you with interesting entrées, but—"

"This vegetable stew wasn't bad," Frank Delaney piped up. "I can live with stuff like this."

Aurelia glanced down at Matthew, who might have been right about the potatoes. He seemed somewhat surprised that she'd taken the offensive today. Good. She didn't want him to think she was incapable of handling her own issues.

"So here's the deal," she said. "I want to challenge you a bit with the entrées, although I'll modify them if I decide they're too off-the-wall, and I'll stick to Mary Lou's recipes for dessert."

The cheer that went up convinced her that she had, in fact, been torturing them with her innovative meals. But they hadn't complained, either because they were good sports or because they'd been afraid they'd end up with nothing to eat. That was about to change.

"From now on, I want you to tell me what you liked and didn't like about the meals," she said. "Don't be shy."

"Okay, what were those things that looked like a piece of pine tree stuck crossways in the stew?" Shorty asked. "It didn't look edible."

"It's rosemary. I used it as a garnish. It flavors the dish but you're not supposed to eat it."

Frank Delaney spoke up. "How are we supposed to know that?"

"Good point. From now on, I'll make an announcement about what's to be eaten and what's not."

Frank nodded. "So we might get some culture while Aurelia's here. That's not so bad."

"Do we have to eat everything on our plate?" The speaker was one of the teenagers, a tall, slim boy named Jeff.

Aurelia didn't know how to answer because she wasn't sure what sort of rules had been set down for the kids. She looked over at the family table where Sarah's fiancé Pete Beckett sat. The tall, distinguished-looking philanthropist was underwriting the program, so he should probably be the authority on cleaning or not cleaning one's plate.

Pete stood. "No, you don't have to eat everything. All I ask is that you *try* everything. Aurelia's right. You have a chance while she's here to expand your food horizons, and I advise you to take advantage of it."

Aurelia smiled at Pete. She'd always liked him and now she liked him even more. He and Sarah would be a positive force for change in the world, and she felt privileged that she'd come to know both of them.

The lunch hour was almost over, so she glanced around at those seated at the tables, her customers, as it were. "Any other questions before you grab that last brownie and take off?"

"Yeah," said the short boy named Lester. "What's for dessert tomorrow?"

"I haven't decided yet."

Lester grinned. "How about more brownies?"

She could imagine how quickly she'd want to slit her wrists if she had to make double chocolate chip brownies every day. "Sorry, but there won't be brownies tomorrow. It'll be something else from Mary Lou's recipes, but not brownies."

Shorty heaved a sigh. "Then we're safe."

When she pinned him with a glance, he held up both hands. "No offense, Aurelia, but the past week has been a menu minefield."

She laughed. It was impossible to be upset with a guy like Shorty. "I'm not taking out all the mines, but I promise to alert you as to where they are. Now I know everybody has work to do, so thanks for staying to listen."

Chairs scooted back and the dining room began to empty. In the process, several people came up to thank her for meeting the situation head-on.

Sarah was one of the last. "You have guts," she said. "I don't know if I would have had the courage to ask a roomful of people if they liked the food I'd been serving them for a week."

"I didn't know I was going to do it until I started tapping on Matthew's glass," Aurelia said. "But now that the subject's out in the open, I feel a hundred times better. And to give credit where credit is due, I wouldn't have been thinking along those lines if it weren't for Matthew." She glanced around. "Where did he go, anyway?"

"He took off," said Emmett, the ranch's foreman. "He has a surprise brewing with Houdini and one of the teenagers and I gather they need all the extra time they can get this afternoon."

"Oh." Aurelia had hoped to talk with him. In fact, she'd looked forward to the opportunity ever since that searing kiss he'd given her, which had been all too brief but had fueled her fantasies, even so.

But she shouldn't be surprised that he was in demand, or that he'd made other friends at the ranch. She could imagine how those teenagers must look up to a man like Matthew, a man so accomplished and a genuinely nice person on top of that.

Some day in the future she'd probably point to him during a TV appearance, and she'd tell whoever was around that she'd spent time with Matthew Tredway. And yes, she'd say, *he is as incredible as he seems on TV. More incredible, actually. And he has the bluest eyes.*

"Let's get the last of these dishes into the dishwasher." Sarah reached for an empty brownie plate.

"I can do the last little bit, Sarah." Aurelia glanced around at the empty dining room. "There's not much left, and I'm sure you and Pete need to take care of details with the teen program."

"Actually, we do have some items to go over," Pete said. "I'm trying to talk Sarah into hiring a housekeeper."

"And I say the boys can learn to do housework, the same as I trained my three." Sarah sounded determined. "Hire a housekeeper and we'll all get lazy."

"I agree the boys should do their share, but this is a huge house and they're only here for the summer." Pete looped an arm around Sarah's shoulders. "I'm selfish.

I want you to spend less time cleaning and more time with me."

"Now there's a man after my own heart," Aurelia said. "I think a housekeeper is a wonderful idea."

Sarah looked uncertain. "It's just that I've been caring for this place most of my life, and—"

"And you don't think anyone else will do it as well," Pete said. "They probably won't, but we'd find the cream of the crop, and you'd train them. And what about the wedding you're putting on at the end of August for Jack's half brother Wyatt? Wouldn't you like help during that time?"

"I suppose." Sarah glanced at Aurelia. "You know what? I don't know if you can get any more time off from the bank, but having you around for that event would be a huge help. Wyatt's mother and father are sort of…"

"Snobs," Pete said.

"I wasn't going to say that."

"No, but it's true. If we had a gourmet cook on hand, that would be a nice touch."

Aurelia had heard a little of the story from Mary Lou. Jack's mother Diana had left the ranch when Jack was a toddler and had never returned. But one of her twin sons, only a few years younger than Jack, had. It had made for some tense times, but now Wyatt was accepted by everyone. Whether his mother would be if she came to the wedding was another story.

"I can check." Aurelia was pleased to be asked. "But I don't know if I can get more time off so soon."

"Well, let us know," Sarah said. "And now we'd better go tackle those applications, Pete."

That reminded Aurelia of something she'd wondered about. "How do boys get into the program? Last time I was in town somebody wanted to know, and I had no idea."

"We take applications from various social-service agencies," Sarah said. "They have access to kids who are in foster care or in dicey home situations who could use a summer of fun mixed with structure and responsibility. Pete and I have talked about creating a website with online applications for anyone who wants to contact us directly, but we also like the filtering system the agencies provide."

Aurelia nodded. "Yeah, with such an awesome program, you could get flooded." She turned to Pete. "And by the way, thanks for the vote of confidence on my food."

"You're welcome. I've only been here for lunch a couple of times since you arrived, and I was impressed by the innovations. I didn't realize until today that others weren't as supportive."

Sarah wrapped an arm around his waist and looked up at him. "You've been busy advocating for the kids." She turned to Aurelia. "Pete wants to make sure that when these eight boys leave here in August with better coping skills, they also have a better support system than when they came. It won't matter what happens at the ranch if they get dumped back in the same environment with no lifelines."

"That's a worthy goal. And speaking of those kids, when I came to fill in for Aunt Mary Lou, I didn't think about the fact I'd be cooking for teenagers. They'd probably rather have pizza and cheeseburgers."

"Don't worry about it," Pete said. "They deserve to have their horizons expanded as much, if not more, than the cowhands. Why not have them look back on this summer and realize it was the first time they'd had gourmet food?"

"Yes," Aurelia said, "but if they hate it—"

"They're not going to hate it." Sarah gave her a look that communicated more than she was saying. "Now you have Matthew on your side."

That look told Aurelia that Sarah had noticed the sparks between the two of them and she had no objection. Aurelia wouldn't get in trouble for having a crush on the sexy horse trainer.

Or, more accurately, she wouldn't get in trouble with Sarah. She could still create problems for herself if she allowed any thoughts of white lace and promises to dance around in her head. If she became involved with Matthew—and that looked increasingly likely—she had to keep her heart strictly out of it.

About three hours later, she wondered if that would be possible. She'd walked down to the corral to see if Matthew was indeed riding Houdini as he'd predicted and found that Lester was perched bareback on the black and white Paint. Lester held the knotted reins in one hand, but for extra insurance, he gripped Houdini's mane with his other as they slowly circled the corral. Matthew had allowed Lester to have the glory of that first ride, and Aurelia's heart squeezed.

The smallest of the teens, Lester hadn't yet found a friend among the other kids. But he'd found a friend in Matthew, and apparently in Houdini, too. Aurelia would bet Lester was now the envy of all seven boys lining the rail. If not for the riding helmet, he would look like a Native American boy who'd just tamed a wild pony.

The stallion seemed proud to be carrying his small passenger as he moved regally along the fence with his head up and his magnificent white tail sweeping behind him. Matthew stood inside the corral, obviously poised to go to the rescue if necessary. His gaze followed the horse's every move, although at one point he glanced at Aurelia and gave her a quick smile.

She smiled back. Befriending Lester and giving him the honor of the first ride on Houdini reinforced what she'd already suspected about Matthew. He liked to help others—both people and animals—succeed. That was a very heartwarming trait.

"Hey, Lester!" yelled Jeff, the tall thin boy who'd spoken up at lunch. "This is boring! Make him run!"

"Keep your voice down," Matthew said. "This is a horse that's never been ridden, and yet Lester's doing it after only a few hours of working with him. If you find that boring, you're welcome to clean out some stalls."

"I thought this would be more exciting," Jeff grumbled. "I want to see him run."

Emmett approached the corral from the barn. "Jeff, you're out of line. Either be quiet or leave the area."

When Jeff's shoulders stiffened, Aurelia crossed her fingers. So far the boys hadn't had any discipline problems, but Jeff was the most troubled and the one most likely to act out. She hoped he wouldn't ruin their perfect record today.

No such luck. Jeff picked up a small rock and threw it at Houdini, hitting him on the rump. The horse bolted, although his ability to run was hampered somewhat by the size of the corral. Still, he was moving fast enough to send Lester flying if he lost his seat.

From the corner of her eye Aurelia saw Emmett collar Jeff, but her attention was riveted by the drama of the boy, the horse and the man standing in the corral.

Matthew's voice rang out, clear and full of confidence. "You're doing great, Lester. Keep a good hold on that mane. Push your fists down against his neck. That's it. Sit up straight. Grip with your legs. Terrific!"

Lester's face was a pale mask of concentration as he followed Matthew's directions to the letter. Even from her position outside the corral, Aurelia could see his white-knuckled grasp of Houdini's mane. But he stayed on the horse.

"Looking good," Matthew said. "Feeling good?"

Lester gave a short, jerky nod.

"Just keep doing what you're doing. Nice straight back, good tight hold on his mane, grip with your legs. We're going to let him run it out. You're fine. Beautiful job." Matthew kept up the positive commentary.

In his place, Aurelia wondered if she would have been able to speak, or if her voice would have been that steady if she could. She didn't think so. She also didn't think Matthew was as calm as he appeared. There was a white line around his mouth that indicated he was controlling his emotions so that he could help Lester.

The boy needed a steady adult voice to talk him through this adventure so he'd come out of it a hero instead of a casualty. Aurelia kept her attention on the boy, and after a few more circuits, he looked a little less scared. A couple more and he began to smile.

Matthew must have noticed it, too. "Having some fun, are you?"

"Yeah! This is cool!"

"You're a natural rider, Lester. So you're feeling good up there?"

"Yep."

"Then let's help Houdini learn from this. We don't want him to think he can just take off like that whenever he feels like it. So when he starts to slow down, I want you to squeeze with your legs and cluck with your tongue to make him canter some more. He stops when you say so, not when he wants to. You're the boss."

"Wow. I like that." Lester sat up even straighter. "And there he goes. Slowing down."

"Squeeze with your lower leg and cluck with your tongue."

Aurelia heard Lester make a clicking sound with his tongue and Houdini immediately started cantering faster as they circled the corral a few more times.

"That's enough," Matthew said. "Now I want you to stop squeezing his sides and start pulling back on the reins and say whoa. I'm going to step into his line of vision and act like a traffic cop. Ready?"

With a nod Lester pulled back on the reins and said, "Whoa, Houdini." Matthew moved into the path Houdini had created and held up both hands, palms forward. "Whoa, Houdini," Lester repeated. "Whoa, boy."

The horse slowed and came to a stop inches from Matthew. His sides heaved as he blew out through flared nostrils.

"Good boy." Matthew took hold of his bridle and patted his neck. "Good boy."

"That was *awesome*." Lester's grin took over his entire face.

Matthew glanced up at him. "Ready to come down now?"

"Sure." He sounded nonchalant about it, but he was trembling.

"Need help?"

"Nope, I'm good." But when he hopped off, he staggered, as if his knees weren't quite up to the job of supporting him. "Just a little wobbly, I guess."

"Adrenaline can do that to you," Matthew said.

"Yeah, that was a *rush,* man." He straightened and walked to where Matthew stood. Then he wrapped his arms around Houdini's neck. "Thanks for not tossing me in the dirt, buddy."

Matthew put a hand on Lester's shoulder. "Great riding. Couldn't have done better myself."

Lester gazed up at him, hero worship shining in his expression. "Thanks, Mr. Tredway."

"Let's take Houdini back to his stall. I think he's had enough training for today."

"And he needs a good rubdown," Lester added as he ducked under the horse's neck and took hold of Houdini's bridle on the other side.

With Matthew on the opposite side, they headed toward the gate. Emmett still had a firm grip on Jeff's shoulder, but one of the other boys rushed to open the gate for them.

As Matthew passed Aurelia, he gave her a tight smile. "Quite a show, huh?"

"It was." She could tell his anger at the boy who'd

thrown the rock simmered under the surface of his apparent calm.

When he passed Jeff, he paused. In a low, icy tone that was far more devastating than yelling would have been, he let Jeff have it. "Anyone who could throw a rock at a horse, especially in a situation like we had today, has no business being on a ranch."

"Don't worry," Emmett said just as quietly. "Jeff won't be staying. I'll take him to see Pete and Sarah to let them know why."

Jeff stared at both of them in disbelief. "But it was just a little rock!"

Matthew's words were laced with fury. "And because you threw it, somebody could have been badly hurt, maybe even killed."

"And that's the crux of it," Emmett added. "You've lost your privilege to stay here." He glanced at the other six boys. "You all get that, right?"

Eyes wide, every boy nodded vigorously.

"Good. I know you're always hungry, so maybe Aurelia will take you to the kitchen and find you a snack."

"I'd be glad to." Aurelia noticed that the boys didn't leap at the suggestion, probably because they were afraid she'd offer them something they didn't want to eat. "Come on, guys," she said. "I have some leftover brownies in the kitchen."

Their cheers were filled with relief as they ran toward the house.

She followed at a more leisurely pace and took a moment to look over at the touching picture Matthew and Lester made as they took Houdini back to the barn. Matthew had turned Lester into a celebrity today, and the boy would never forget it. Besides being gorgeous, Matthew was good with both kids and animals. From what she'd seen so far, she was going to have to work extra hard not to fall in love with him.

6

MATTHEW ATE A halfway decent-tasting plate of spaghetti with the guys in the bunkhouse, although he couldn't help imagining how Aurelia could have improved on the basic recipe. But he was a guest in the bunkhouse, and he wasn't about to complain. It had been Shorty's night to cook, and spaghetti was his usual contribution.

A bottle of wine would have been nice, but the cowhands weren't into it, so Matthew drank the beer they handed him.

"So where did you come from originally?" Tucker asked Matthew as they finished up the last of the spaghetti.

"I was born in Billings," Matthew said.

"You still have family up there?"

"Not anymore." Matthew hadn't been lucky in that respect. His mom had died when he was seven, and his dad, who had sold the ranch after she died, had never recovered emotionally from her death. He'd passed away two years ago, leaving Matthew pretty much without family connections since he had no brothers or sisters and hadn't ever been close to his aunts and uncles. It was a sad little story, and since Shorty didn't press the issue, Matthew chose not to tell it.

Frank picked up a paper napkin and wiped spaghetti sauce from his mustache. Apparently Sarah's rule about paper napkins didn't apply down here. "Everybody's talking about that kid riding Houdini," Frank said. "Who would have thought that horse would let a kid get up on him?"

"I think it was real smart." Bob sat back in his chair and adjusted his glasses. "Risky, but smart. That boy's lighter than any of us, and putting him on bareback meant bypassing the saddle issue."

"But you'll have to deal with the saddle issue sooner or later." Shorty stood. "Everybody done here? I'm ready to clear the table and play some cards."

Matthew stood and picked up his plate. "I'd like to find an English saddle. Start with that."

"It's a good idea." Danny scratched one of his over-sized ears. "That way you give him something that doesn't feel much like the one that scared him before. I'd check with Sarah, see if she knows anybody who has one. I'll bet she does."

"I'll ask her." Matthew stacked his plate on a couple of others and walked into the kitchen.

"Pete took that Jeff kid back to his foster home tonight," Tucker said as he opened the dishwasher.

Matthew inhaled a deep breath. "I can't say I'm sorry."

"Nobody is." Shorty located a cigar and stuck it behind his ear. "Pete being Pete, he's getting the kid into counseling, but we can't have that kind of behavior around here."

"No." Every time Matthew replayed the scene in his head, it ran in slow motion as Jeff leaned down, picked up a rock and hurled it at the horse. If it really had been in slow motion, Matthew could have intercepted the rock. In reality, the rock had been airborne before he could move to stop it.

From that point on, he'd had to clamp down on his anger so that he could be the voice of reason for Lester, who had been terrified at first. The fact that the incident had ended with no injuries didn't change the way Matthew felt about Jeff's behavior.

"So." Shorty grabbed a dish towel and wiped off the table. "I hope you're all prepared to lose tonight, because I'm feeling extremely lucky."

"I can play for a while," Matthew said, "but I'm going up to the house a little before eight." Now he wished Aurelia had said seven, which was only about fifteen minutes from now.

"For what?" Jeb asked.

"I'm going to help Aurelia plan some menus for you guys." It was the story he would stick with until someone figured out there was more going on than menu-planning. They probably would sooner or later. He helped Tucker finish loading the dishwasher and returned to the table.

"Right. Menu-planning. That's a good thing." Jeb set the cards and a tray of chips on the table. "Her speech today was encouraging, but I'm glad you're going to supervise. Don't let her give us any more innards, okay?"

"I won't."

"Or eels," Tucker said. "That was a really bad day."

Matthew winced. It would be a rare cowboy who would get excited about having eels for lunch.

Jeb divided up the chips. "I heard her say something to Sarah about squid, too, but I guess that didn't fly, because we never did get squid for lunch. Probably too expensive. From what I gather, Aurelia's made friends with a chef in Jackson who helps her find bargains on this stuff."

"Don't worry. I'll protect your interests," Matthew said.

"I'll drink to that," Shorty said. "Who wants another beer?"

"No, thanks." Matthew returned to his seat and arranged his chips. "I need to keep a clear head if I'm going to fight the menu wars." He made it sound like a chore that he'd taken on to be noble, when it was anything but.

He was counting the minutes until he could walk up to the house. He'd showered and changed clothes before dinner, but he'd made sure he wasn't too duded up, which would arouse suspicion that this was more like a date than an obligation. Nobody at the table had to know about the condom he'd tucked in his pocket, either.

"See that?" Jeb said. "He's sacrificing his drinking time so that he can do this for us. That's what I call dedication."

"Yeah," Bob said. "Thanks, Matthew."

"Don't mention it." And if they continued to praise him for his sacrifice, he was liable to start feeling guilty. "Glad to help out." They had no idea how glad.

"Those brownies were outstanding." Shorty lit his

cigar. "See if you can talk her into making something like that again. Chocolate always works. Mary Lou has this chocolate cupcake recipe that always went over big. And chocolate pie with whipped cream's another winner. Which reminds me, what we got for dessert?"

Jeb started dealing the cards. "Double Stuf Oreos."

Shorty pushed back his chair. "I'll get 'em. They may not be homemade, but they beat the hell out of roasted figs."

As the poker game got going, there was more talk about the bizarre food Aurelia had insisted on fixing for a solid week, until Matthew had arrived to save the day. He blamed part of this situation on Mary Lou, who should have been clearer about what cowboys would and wouldn't eat. But Mary Lou had been preoccupied with other things, apparently, like getting married and taking the first cruise of her life.

Playing cards helped fill the time until Matthew could leave, but it wasn't fascinating enough to make him forget that he would soon have Aurelia within kissing distance. Whenever he thought about that, he inevitably threw away a winning hand because he wasn't paying attention.

Finally Bob commented on his lack of concentration. "Listen, I hope you're not putting pressure on yourself about this menu business. We can survive another two weeks of her cooking, especially if she does what she said and makes the kind of desserts we're used to."

"I know you can survive." Matthew looked up at the battery-operated clock on the wall and saw with immense relief that he could finally leave. "But I'll give it my best shot." He stood and pushed his chips toward Jeb, who was the banker tonight. "You can divide these up."

"I'll hold them for you," Jeb said. "I figure you'll be back in an hour or so."

"Maybe, maybe not." Matthew didn't think an hour would be nearly enough time for what he had in mind. "Go ahead and divide up my chips. That way if I'm making progress I won't feel like I have to rush back to the game." He couldn't believe he actually said that with a straight face.

"Okay, your call. And good luck."

"Thanks." Grabbing his hat from a well-used rack on the wall, Matthew pushed open the screen door and stepped into the night. As he walked up to the main house and breathed in a lungful of cool air, he wondered if Aurelia had been anticipating their meeting as much as he had. His ego wanted to believe that she had.

This morning when he'd gone looking for Aurelia, he'd come in through the front door because that's how he'd entered the house the night before. But later he'd realized that the back door made more sense. No reason to tromp through the house in his boots and alert everyone that he'd arrived, or conversely, that he was leaving, especially if he left on the late side.

So he bypassed the steps leading up to the front porch and circled around to the rear, where he easily found the back door marked by a yellow porch light. A small deck fanned out to the left, with two rattan chairs inviting anyone working hard in the kitchen to take a break.

Climbing the steps, he rapped on the wooden frame

of the screen door. By his calculations it was exactly eight o'clock.

Light footsteps approached from inside, and Aurelia peeked out. "Oh! You came around this way!" She pushed open the door in welcome.

"It seemed to make more sense. I didn't want to make a grand entrance. Or a grand exit, for that matter."

"Tonight it doesn't matter. Sarah and Pete took the boys to the movies in Jackson. They won't be home 'til late."

"Oh." That was welcome news.

Whatever room he was walking into was lit only by the porch light from outside and a shaft of light from the kitchen beyond. It was enough for him to see that her luxurious golden hair curled around her shoulders instead of being caught up in a ponytail as it had been earlier today.

She'd changed clothes, too. Instead of a T-shirt and jeans, she had on a lacy blouse and capris. She'd even abandoned her running shoes for cute little sandals. Maybe she'd done all that for him. He hoped so.

"This isn't a bad plan," she said. "But it means coming in through the laundry room. I hope you don't mind."

"Nope." As his eyes adjusted to the dim light, he noticed a couple of large washers paired up with companion dryers. The air smelled of warm fabric and soap, as if the washers and dryers had been used recently. But he also picked up the scent of warm woman.

This morning she'd absorbed all the fragrances of the kitchen at breakfast time, a combination of coffee, hot buttered toast and bacon. He'd enjoyed that, especially when he'd kissed her. At lunch she'd brought all the ratatouille herbs and spices with her when she'd leaned down to set his plate in front of him, and he'd wanted to taste her instead of the food.

But tonight her aroma reminded him of a mountain meadow filled with wildflowers, which meant she'd showered before this meeting, same as he had. His heart rate picked up as he came to the obvious conclusion that tonight was significant for her, too.

Coming in through the back door and standing with her in the subdued light of the laundry room created a feeling of intimacy and stealth, as if they'd planned a secret rendezvous. His body stirred. He'd always been a sucker for atmosphere.

She turned and started into the kitchen. "I have all my cookbooks spread out on the table. I have an idea about what to serve, but you can tell me if it will work."

He hadn't realized that he'd reached for her until he made contact. His hand closed over her shoulder and she went very still. Then a fine tremor ran through her.

His throat was tight with longing. "Aurelia."

Slowly she turned back to him. "I think…" She swallowed. "I think we should plan the menu before…"

"You're right." Tossing his hat on the nearest dryer, he stepped forward and drew her into his arms. Because she was so much shorter than he was, he had to lift her up onto her tiptoes. "You're absolutely right." Giving in to the needs that had tormented him all day, he captured that full, sweet mouth in a kiss that made his ears ring.

She tasted of mint toothpaste and he quickly decided it was his favorite. Their first kiss had been hard and fast, with no time for him to use his tongue. But this time…her mouth softened under his as if she wanted his invasion.

Groaning, he thrust his tongue into the moist, minty recesses of her delicious mouth. The contact made him dizzy with wanting her. She was heaven in his arms, her lush, rounded body pressed against his with no sharpness, no angles, just a banquet of enticing female curves.

Sliding her hands up his chest, she linked them behind his neck and wiggled closer. The movement drove him slightly crazy. Before he realized it, he'd pulled her blouse up and unfastened her bra.

When it came loose, she stopped kissing him for a moment and leaned back. He paused, worried that she'd ask him to stop. The pressure building behind his fly would become a major problem if she did.

"Matthew?" She gulped for air.

"Yes?" His breathing wasn't all that steady, either, and his heart galloped like a runaway stallion.

"Does this mean we'll do our menu-planning later?"

He choked out a laugh. "I hope so."

"In that case…" Unclasping her hands from around his neck, she stepped back. Grabbing the hem of her blouse, she pulled it over her head and lobbed it onto one of the dryers. Then she stripped off her bra and sent that sailing after the blouse. "Better?"

He nodded mutely, transfixed by the glory that was Aurelia. Even in the shadowy light, his first glimpse of her breasts nearly made him come. Full and perfect, they trembled delicately with each quivering breath. Beneath his gaze, her nipples tightened, and his mouth grew moist with a basic need to savor what she offered.

"I hope you don't think I'm too bold."

"How could I? I started this." And their spontaneously chosen location was brilliant, he realized now. Spanning her waist with both hands, he lifted her on top of the nearest dryer.

Her breasts swayed, and as he cupped them in both hands, he drew in a quick breath, overcome by the sensuous delight of holding her. "You're magnificent."

She arched into his hands. "I'm glad you're pleased."

"I want to please *you*." Cradling her breasts, he stroked his thumbs across her nipples. "Tell me what you like."

She covered his hands with hers. "I like the erotic feel of your big hands, calloused with work, stroking my skin." She closed her eyes. "While you're touching me like this, I can imagine all the ways you use these strong, hard-working fingers, and all the ways you could use them to bring me pleasure…squeezing gently, kneading…that's so good, Matthew. Mmm. So good."

Leaning forward, he nibbled her mouth. "I should have known."

Her response was throaty, seductive. "Known what?"

"That you'd be like this, so sensual." He continued to massage her breasts as he nuzzled her throat. "So ready to be loved."

She tilted her head back, giving him greater access. "Why?"

"You're passionate about food." Kissing his way across her collarbone, he nipped gently at her shoulder. "Food and sex…our basic needs." Anticipation made his voice quiver as he moved down the slope of one breast. "At least, they're mine." At last he reached his destination and drew one furled nipple into his mouth.

Moaning softly, she took his head in her hands and arched her back, holding him to her breast. "Yes," she whispered. "Mine, too. Oh, mine, too."

His erection strained against his zipper as he lavished attention on her breasts. Releasing her hold on his head, she braced her arms behind her and thrust her chest forward, begging for more. Her hips shifted restlessly on the smooth enamel surface.

He noticed, and took satisfaction in that impatient, wiggling motion. She wanted him as frantically as he wanted her.

He hadn't experienced this level of wild lust in years, and it felt good to want so much that his control was starting to slip. Gasping, he released her. "I want more."

Her rapid breathing making her breasts jiggle, she gazed up at him. "Meaning?"

Silently he pulled the condom from his pocket.

Her mouth curved in a purely feminine smile. "I didn't know you were packing."

"Insulted?"

"Oh, no." She unbuttoned her capris and starting wiggling out of them. "Not at all."

7

AURELIA HAD ALWAYS been grateful for her body even if it wasn't designed for high fashion. Tonight she was even more grateful, because Matthew seemed mesmerized by her curves. He'd reacted to her like a man dying of thirst confronted with a bubbling fountain. He couldn't seem to get enough.

He helped her pull off her panties and her capris, but in the process he stopped to kiss her thighs, her knees, her calves and even her toes when he slipped off her sandals. She'd never had a man pay such worshipful attention in her life. He hadn't been able to see and appreciate her sexy undies, but he obviously hadn't needed the extra boost to his libido. He was wild for her.

Then again, she was wild for him, too. She'd never tossed her clothes away with such abandon on only the second day after meeting someone. But Matthew wouldn't be around long, and she didn't want to waste time building up to what promised to be an outstanding sexual experience.

Once he'd dispensed with her clothes, he reached for the buckle on his belt.

"Wait." She splayed her hand against his powerful chest, which heaved with eagerness. "I want to touch you, too. Let me…" Instead of finishing the sentence, she grasped the open collar of his shirt in both hands and pulled.

Snaps gave way like exploding popcorn to reveal the spectacular pecs and abs she'd seen outlined by his tight T-shirt this morning. Pulling the shirttails from the waist of his jeans, she spread the material open and slid her hands from his taut stomach upward. She encountered passion-warmed skin, springy dark hair and flat nipples.

She touched him lightly, teasingly, fascinated with the way he quivered as she explored with her fingers. "Are you ticklish?"

"No, I'm about to explode." His voice was tight. "I haven't had a problem with premature ejaculation since I was sixteen. But with you, I'm worried."

She massaged his pecs. "You really think you'll come while I do this?"

"It's not so much that, although I like it." His voice was like sandpaper, and he cleared his throat. "Your breasts jiggle when you stroke me and that's…driving me slowly insane."

"Oh." She drew her hands back. "Wouldn't want you to go crazy."

"I appreciate that." He reached for his belt buckle again. "Now?"

"Okay," she said softly, her gaze focused on what he was about to unveil. She wanted what was inside his jeans, wanted it very much. She only hoped she could handle him. He was a very big guy.

Then he unzipped his fly and shoved down his briefs, and she realized that he was, indeed, a *very* big guy. Her little gasp must have alerted him to her concern, because he glanced up before tearing open the condom package. "I'll go slow," he said.

"I trust you." Considering the ache of longing he'd created with all his kisses and urgent touching, she had to trust him. She needed him deep inside her as much as he needed to be there. They'd have to work it out.

His fingers shook a little as he put on the condom. "I can't believe how much I want you."

"The feeling's mutual."

He snapped the condom into place and cupped her face in his big hands. "That's nice to know." He kissed her with a restraint that made him quiver, and then he lifted his mouth from hers. "I promise not to hurt you."

"I'm not worried." But she was, a little. Still, the prize was worth the risk.

"Scoot forward."

She did, her bottom sliding easily over the top of the dryer. "You'd better hold on to me or I'm liable to skate right across this surface like a hockey puck on an icy pond."

His grin flashed in the dim light. "Oh, I'm going to hold on to you, Aurelia." His voice was rich with promise and desire. "I'm going to make sure we stay well and truly connected until we both have the orgasm we're looking forward to."

That was the sort of confident boast that thrilled her right down to her already tingling toes.

Grasping her thighs in his large, capable hands, he took a deep breath. "You can hold on to me, too."

"Where?" Her hand hovered over his impressive johnson.

"Not there."

"Oh."

"Hold on to my arms."

She clutched his straining biceps. "Gotcha."

"Easy does it." Drawing her closer to the edge, he probed with that amazing piece of equipment and sighed. "You're drenched."

"Can't help it."

"Nice compliment." He rocked forward a little and drew in a sharp breath. "This is going to be good."

"Mmm." She thought so, too, once she got used to the sheer girth of him.

"You okay?"

"Uh-huh."

His breathing was labored as he eased forward. "Stop me if you…ah, please don't tell me to stop."

"Don't stop." As he slid deeper, she began to reap the benefits as he came in contact with every vibrating nerve ending in that sensitive channel. She had to agree with him. This was going to be good. Very good.

Slowly he sank up to the hilt. She wouldn't have believed it was possible, but she'd taken every bit of his length inside her so-willing body. Amazingly, they were a perfect fit.

If she tightened around him the slightest bit, her body responded with waves of pleasure that could lead to a climax in no time. He wouldn't even have to move.

She clenched her muscles again and felt the beginnings of an orgasm.

He groaned. "Nice."

"Stay still, and I can just—"

"That's no fun." He eased back.

"But you wouldn't even have to move."

"But I want to, Aurelia." He shoved deep again and withdrew.

Her body vibrated, poised to erupt at any moment.

He began to pump slowly. "I love stroking back and forth, listening to those little whimpers you're making."

She hadn't even realized she was doing it.

"You can make yourself come, but I'd rather do the honors for you."

And was he ever. He took over the controls, creating a steady friction that coaxed whimpers, moans and gasps from her as he led her relentlessly toward a release that promised to eclipse anything she'd ever experienced.

She felt it building, a tsunami that drew closer, and closer yet. He quickened the pace and kept to his vow of holding her steady despite his urgent stroking.

"Come now," he murmured. "Let go, Aurelia. Let it happen."

As if she had a choice. Arching upward, she came apart, and he caught her cries by covering her mouth. Even though they were alone, he obviously wanted to be careful that they weren't heard. He sustained the rhythm until she sank back against the smooth top of the dryer, sated with pleasure.

Then it was his turn, and he buried himself firmly inside her as the spasms rocked his massive body. Wrenching his mouth away from hers, he pressed it against her shoulder to muffle his deep groans of satisfaction.

They stayed that way for several minutes as their breathing slowed and sanity returned. Aurelia pried her fingers from Matthew's arms and hoped she hadn't left a mark he'd have trouble explaining later.

Matthew rubbed her thighs where he'd been clutching her and seemed to have the same concern. "I hope I didn't leave any bruises."

She drew a shaky breath. "If you did, no one will see them but you. I don't wear shorts when I'm working."

He leaned his forehead against hers. "Are you saying that we can do this again sometime?"

"If you're interested."

He chuckled. "I think you know the answer to that."

That warmed her. She'd thought he'd had a pretty good time, but she liked hearing it, anyway. "We might want to change the venue next time, though."

He lifted his head to gaze at her, even though visibility was limited in the unlit room. "Honestly, this isn't the way I intended tonight to go. I thought we'd figure out a menu first, and then maybe have a little wine, and then...see what happened."

She laughed. "You were picturing something more normal, like a bed?"

"As a matter of fact, I was. I know you have one in your apartment."

"I had the same idea." She cupped his face in her hands. "But it's flattering to think that you couldn't wait."

"It's embarrassing. The minute I was alone with you in a darkened room, I started kissing you."

"You notice I didn't offer any objections." She combed her fingers through his hair. "I knew this was likely to happen, but I wasn't sure how it would play out."

He heaved a sigh. "Considering that I've been fantasizing about you since we met, tonight was a foregone conclusion, but doing it in the laundry room might not be the classiest move I've ever made."

"Oh, I don't know." She leaned forward and dropped a quick kiss on his mouth. "It's an original way to kick off a fling."

He was silent for a moment. "It's probably good you brought that up. I'd meant to, but I got carried away before we had any chance to talk."

"Look, Matthew, you're an internationally known horseman who travels the globe for your job. I'm a bank teller who loves to cook but hates to travel. A fling is all we could ever have, given those circumstances."

"I'm glad we agree on that."

"I knew it from the moment I started having inappropriate thoughts about your body."

That made him laugh. "And when was that, exactly?"

"When you first walked through the kitchen door yesterday."

"That's about the same time I started having inappropriate thoughts about your body, too."

"And isn't it nice that we can agree to enjoy each other without getting tangled up in obligations?"

"Yes." He stroked his hands along her thighs. "Yes, it is. Our only obligation is to plan some menus together."

"Which we should probably do now."

He sighed. "I suppose. And we can't stay in the laundry room forever." But he didn't move away.

"No."

"At some point I have to disengage from your warm and inviting body."

"Yes." But she missed him the moment he did. There was a feeling of rightness to that connection that had no business being so perfect. They had no future. But, she had to admit, they had one heck of a present.

TWENTY MINUTES LATER, Matthew gazed at Aurelia across the small kitchen table and tried to concentrate on something besides the gentle rise and fall of her breasts under the green lacy top and the perfect bow of her upper lip, which he longed to trace with his tongue. He'd chosen to sit across the table from her because sitting beside her was definitely going to lead to more touching, kissing and fondling, and he'd only brought one condom.

When he'd told her, she'd kidded him about his low expectations. Then she'd sweetly suggested he could go back to the bunkhouse and fetch some more. But he couldn't get away with that kind of expedition while the guys were still awake and playing poker.

So they were planning the next day's lunch menu, as he'd promised the cowhands he would do. It was important, after all, because planning successful menus would guarantee him the right to come back to see Aurelia every night. Next time he'd bring more than one condom.

"Poulet demi-deuil." Aurelia pointed to the picture in the cookbook. "It means—"

"I know. Chicken in partial mourning. It's the partial mourning that's going to get you into trouble. Even if you can get the black truffles—"

"I can. I've found a gourmet market in Jackson that has all sorts of great ingredients."

"But if you tuck those black truffles under the skin of the roasted chicken like the recipe says, every cowboy in the room, with the possible exception of Pete, who's fairly sophisticated, will think that chicken has mange. Or it's somehow decaying and you haven't noticed."

"I can tell them it's only black truffles. And they'll learn something new."

"Aurelia, there are certain colors that don't work with your average cowboy when it comes to food. Black is one of them. When he sees black food, he assumes it's either burnt or it's gone bad. It's a mind-set that you'll have trouble changing."

Her beautiful mouth formed the cutest little pout. If he left his chair and went over there, he could get rid of that pout and have a great time doing it. But they wouldn't get the menu planned, and after they'd kissed and carried on, all without any satisfaction for him because he was without a second condom, she might go ahead with the chicken in partial mourning that she was so set on.

Then he'd get slammed for not being able to influence her food choices. If he couldn't do that, people might question what business he had coming up here every night, and the whole program would be in jeopardy. So he couldn't leave his chair and kiss away her pout.

"Use regular mushrooms instead of the black truffles and then you'll be okay," he said. "Oh, and where it tells you to puree all the veggies and pour them on the platter? Don't puree the veggies. The guys will think you're giving them baby food."

Aurelia propped her chin on her fist and stared at him. "Then it's not the same dish."

"No, but it's not fried chicken and potato salad, either."

"You're no fun, Matthew."

He smiled at her. "That isn't what you said in the laundry room."

Her cheeks turned pink. "Okay, you're fun in that respect, but when it comes to cooking, you're a total wet blanket."

"It's my job."

"I think they'd be fascinated by the black truffles."

"Sure they would, as long as you didn't serve them for lunch. When a man's been mucking out stalls all morning, it's best not to startle him with what's on his plate for lunch. He wants something he recognizes, and black truffles don't qualify."

"Okay, okay!" She held up her hands in surrender. "I'll make it with regular mushrooms and I won't puree the veggies. I can see your point about that part. A grown man doesn't want his veggies put through a blender as if he has no teeth to chew with."

"Now you're getting the idea. By the way, will the boys be eating dinner here tomorrow night?"

"Yes."

"What are you going to serve them?" Matthew figured he might as well cover that base while he was at it.

"Bifteck marchand de vin."

"I get the wine and steak part of that, but what's the *marchand* in it?"

"It's shallot-red-wine sauce."

"Mmm." Matthew could almost taste it. "Wish I could have some of that tomorrow night."

"Come on up. I'm sure Sarah wouldn't care, and the boys would love it."

He considered that for a moment. "I think I'd better eat down at the bunkhouse. The guys like the fact that I'm hanging out down there, and if I started coming up here to eat dinner, I don't know how that would go over. But I wouldn't object if you saved me a little bit to taste."

"I can do that. So you approve of my dinner menu for the kids, then?"

"I think they'll like it fine."

"I can have yours ready when you get here." She gave him a slow smile. "You want it sliced and made into a tender little sandwich? Or juicy and hot?"

"Why do I get the feeling you're not talking about the steak?"

"Would I do that?"

"I think you might. And I think…" He forgot what he'd been about to say when her foot slid up his leg and across his thigh to settle against his crotch. "What are you doing, Aurelia Imogene?"

"Nothing."

But she was definitely doing something. She'd slipped off her sandal and was rubbing the ball of her foot over his zipper. She was getting a rise out of him, too.

Reaching down, he caught her foot and held it still. "Don't tease."

"You don't like it?"

"I would love it if I'd brought more supplies, but I didn't, so you're torturing me for nothing."

"For someone who's traveled the world, you don't have much imagination when it comes to sex."

"You don't know me well enough to make that claim."

"That could be true." Pulling her foot free, she scooted down in her chair. "Maybe I should get to know you better."

"I don't know what you're talking about."

"Then let me demonstrate." In no time she'd disappeared under the table, and next thing he knew, she was kneeling under it and had a hold on his zipper.

"Aurelia." He leaned over and peered at her. "Come out of there."

"I will in a minute." She pulled his zipper down and reached inside his jeans.

"Hey." He caught her wrist. "Stop that."

"But I think you would really like it." She fondled him with her other hand. "I'm no expert at this, but I can probably give you a great memory to take back to the bunkhouse."

Sitting up again so he had better balance, he grabbed that wrist, too. "I already have a great memory of you having an orgasm on the dryer."

Her voice lowered into a soft purr of seduction. "Then how about a great memory of me giving you an orgasm under the kitchen table? This might be your one and only chance, because tomorrow night the house will be full of people again."

He was trying mightily to resist, but the more she talked, the harder he became.

She leaned down and rubbed her cheek against the cotton of his briefs, which were barely restraining his bad boy. "You say no, but this part of you says yes."

"You're crazy." As the ache for her grew stronger, his resistance weakened.

"Earlier you said I was passionate."

"Crazy and passionate."

She nuzzled him through the cotton material. "I want you," she murmured. "I want to lick and nibble and suck and—"

Groaning softly, he let go of her wrists. He was only human, and she was…ah, she was making love to the tip of his penis. His eyes nearly rolled back in his head at the sensation. He had a clear mental image of her plump mouth, and as he thought of it closing over that sensitive part of him, he almost came right then.

But now that he'd surrendered, he wanted it to last longer than a few seconds. That wasn't going to be easy as she dipped one hand inside the opening of his briefs and cupped his family jewels. She might not be an expert at oral sex, but she had good instincts. Soon he had to grip the edge of the table and clench his jaw to keep from moaning out loud at the pleasure she was giving him.

With one hand fondling his twins, one stroking his shaft, and her mouth and tongue very busy playing him like a flute, he knew this ecstasy wouldn't last long. His orgasm rolled closer, stealing his breath and kicking his heart into high gear. Then she did some swirly thing with her tongue and took him all the way to the back of her throat.

Squeezing his eyes shut and choking back his cry of

release, he erupted. Boldly she caressed him, milking him of all he had to give until the tremors gradually faded. He slumped in his chair with his eyes closed, and wondered if he could just stay there for the night, or maybe for the next week or two. He wasn't sure how soon he'd be capable of moving.

Vaguely he realized that she'd tucked his happy penis back inside his briefs and zipped his fly. He lost track of her whereabouts after that, but she must have climbed out from under the table, because now she was leaning over him and kissing his cheek.

"Thanks for the menu-planning session," she murmured in his ear. "I think it's time for you to go back to the bunkhouse, unless you want to spend the night in my bed and say to heck with what people think when they find out."

Taking a long, slow breath, he opened his eyes and looked up at her. "You are an amazing woman, Aurelia Imogene Smith."

She smiled. "That's the orgasm talking."

"Nope." Planting his palms flat on the table, he pushed himself to his feet. "That's experience talking." He drew her into his arms. "I'm not exactly a virgin, you know. I have some basis for comparison, and you are amazing. After knowing you for twenty-four hours, I'm prepared to be your sex slave."

Tilting her head, she looked up at him. "Come back tomorrow night and I'll take you up on that."

"Wild horses wouldn't keep me away."

8

AURELIA MADE THE CHICKEN with regular mushrooms instead of black truffles, but once again, she couldn't call the dish by its proper name because Matthew had talked her into stripping the meaning right out of it. The chicken was no longer in partial mourning. It looked pretty much like any roasted chicken would.

She'd figured out years ago that she wasn't good at art, music or writing. But cooking satisfied her urge to bring something new and useful into the world, especially when the final result was beautiful or interesting. This chicken didn't qualify on either account.

Still, the warmth of Matthew's gaze whenever she caught him watching her during lunch was worth bastardizing as many recipes as necessary. Several of the hands and a couple of the teenagers came up after lunch to compliment her on the meal.

She wasn't sure if they were doing it on their own or if Matthew had prompted them, but either way, she was happy about their comments. If they genuinely liked the food, then she was making progress. If they were only following Matthew's directions, his support meant the world to her and she could be happy about that, too.

He found a moment during lunch to invite her back down to the corral this afternoon to watch him work with Lester and Houdini. He said some of the other boys would be included today, as well. She cleaned up the kitchen in record time so she could do that.

When she arrived, six teenagers lined the fence rail instead of seven. Emmett wasn't around, nor was his daughter Emily, who often helped with the boys. But the tall, dark-haired cowboy named Tucker was there to supervise. Inside the corral, Matthew stood back while Lester held an English saddle out to Houdini and talked to him about it.

Aurelia joined Tucker at the railing. "How come they're using an English saddle instead of a Western one?" Aurelia didn't know a lot about horsemanship, but she recognized the difference in saddles.

"That's Matthew's idea. Houdini had a bad experience with a Western saddle." Tucker tipped his hat back. "Sarah called his former owners this morning, and sure enough, when they had Houdini their son was about Lester's size and he spent a lot of time with the horse."

"So that's why Houdini took so quickly to Lester."

Tucker nodded. "That's the theory. Houdini seems to trust him. I'm not saying he doesn't trust Matthew, because I think he does, but his preference seems to be for Lester. Matthew's smart enough to use that."

"And Lester's obviously having the time of his life."

"Yeah." Tucker grinned. "If he keeps this up and becomes Houdini's best friend, he'll probably end up with a job here once he's old enough."

"I'm gonna get a job here when I'm old enough," said the boy standing closest to Tucker.

Aurelia recognized Gary, a chubby boy with brown hair and freckles.

Gary's comment was followed by the others piping up with "Me, too."

"It's a great place to work," Tucker said. "I've been here since last fall, and I love it." He pointed to the black and white Paint in the corral. "Fortunately that horse didn't cost me my job last Christmas."

That got everybody's attention. Aurelia and the boys listened in fascination as Tucker described Houdini's Christmas Eve escape from the barn right before a blizzard.

"It was my fault that he got out, so I went after him on a snowmobile, which I wrecked, but I caught the horse. Then the blizzard hit."

Gary was wide-eyed. "Then what?"

"An angel rescued me and Houdini."

"A real angel?"

Tucker laughed. "I think she is, but she claims she's not. Her name's Lacey, and we're getting married this Christmas Eve."

"Wow." Gary glanced into the corral. "You should probably invite Houdini to the wedding."

"I probably should at that. Now that Matthew and Lester are teaching him manners, I might be able to find a way to work him into the celebration. There's no doubt that horse was our matchmaker."

"Then I'm glad he's being trained," Aurelia said. "Maybe Matthew should see how he does with a sleigh if you're having a Christmas Eve wedding." She leaned against the top rail of the fence as she pictured a romantic ceremony with pine boughs and mistletoe.

She hoped to have a romantic wedding someday, but she hadn't met the man she'd want to spend her life with. Well, except maybe the man in the corral, but he was out of the question. For the first time, though, she admitted to herself that she wished their circumstances were different.

"A sleigh would be cool," Tucker said. "And I really am glad Houdini's going to be a permanent part of the ranch. Until they decided to hire Matthew, they considered selling him."

"That would have been a shame." In more ways than one, she thought. Houdini had brought Matthew here.

"They don't give up on people and animals that easy around here," Tucker said. "That's why it's called the Last Chance."

"They gave up on Jeff," one of the other boys said.

"Not exactly," Tucker said. "You can't keep a boy around who would throw a rock at a horse. Jeff wasn't ready to be here. But Pete, I mean, Mr. Beckett, is getting Jeff some help. They haven't totally given up on Jeff, either."

"Think he'll come back?" Gary asked.

"Not this summer. But maybe someday. I'm sure Mr. Beckett will keep track of him."

"Look!" Gary pointed toward the corral. "Lester's putting the saddle on Houdini!"

With that, everyone seemed to forget about Jeff as they watched Houdini being saddled for the first time since he'd arrived at the ranch. Matthew stood at his head, holding his bridle and talking to him while Lester

kept up a steady stream of conversation as he tightened
the cinch. Houdini turned to look at the boy, but other-
wise he didn't seem particularly worried about having
the saddle on his back.

"Tighten it, and wait till he lets out some air," Matthew said. "Then tighten it some more. Don't want it
swinging around under his belly."

Lester followed Matthew's directions to the letter.
"I think that's got it, Mr. Tredway."

"Ready to climb on?"

"Yep."

"I think we could use another helper. Gary, how
about you?"

"I'm on it, Mr. Tredway." His chest puffed out with
pride, Gary slipped through the rails into the corral.
"Whatcha need?"

"Lace your hands together and give Lester a leg up
while I keep a hold on Houdini's bridle."

He was so very patient. Aurelia couldn't help thinking what a great father he'd make, but a wife and kids
didn't fit his current lifestyle. She'd be doing both of
them a disservice if she started weaving fantasies about
Matthew as a family man.

She had trouble not doing that, though, as she
watched him work with Lester.

"I think it's Lester's voice, too," Tucker said. "You
see how Houdini's ears are always going, picking up
the sound. I don't know what he'll do once Matthew
climbs on."

"Is he going to do that today?" Aurelia felt a shiver
of dread. She knew Matthew risked his safety all the

time while working with horses, but she didn't have to like the idea of him being thrown.

"Not today. Maybe not even tomorrow. But eventually Houdini has to accept the weight of a grown man. He won't always be ridden by a kid."

"I just hope he's careful."

Tucker glanced at her. "You like him, don't you?"

Aurelia felt a blush coming on. "He's a nice guy."

"Yeah, he is." Smiling, Tucker looked away again.

"What?"

"Oh, nothing. Just that Matthew's sleeping in Watkins' old bunk, and Watkins was sweet on the cook. It's just interesting, that's all."

"Hmm." Aurelia had no idea how to respond. She wasn't about to confirm or deny anything at this point.

"Yep." Tucker nodded again, still smiling. "Interesting."

"I'LL BE HEADING BACK up to the house again tonight around eight," Matthew announced as the cowhands sat down to eat the tuna casserole Danny had made.

"Is that right?" Tucker exchanged a grin with Shorty. "What a surprise."

"Well, isn't that what we agreed I'd do? Go up there and check out the menu plans for the next day?"

"We certainly did." Shorty took a swig of his beer. "And you've done an outstanding job. The chicken today was recognizable and even tasted pretty good. I made a point to tell Aurelia about it, too."

"Good. I'm sure she appreciated that." Matthew dug into his tuna casserole but thought about the steak with shallot-red-wine sauce waiting for him up at the house, and the woman who'd offered to serve it juicy and hot. Tuna casserole didn't stand much of a chance against that, but Matthew planned to eat enough to be polite.

"Apparently it takes a lot of discussion to plan something like that chicken dish," Tucker said.

"I was thinking that, too." Behind his wire-framed glasses, Bob's eyes reflected amusement. "You must have to do some tough negotiating."

Matthew shrugged in an attempt to act casual. "Not really. I mean, she suggests something, and then we figure out how to make it a little less gourmet. It's a process."

"A *long* process," Shorty said.

"Unusually long," Frank added as he forked up a bite of the casserole. "Hell, I think I could hammer out the Treaty of Versailles in the time it takes you two to come up with a roasted chicken recipe."

"And dinner tonight for the kids. We had to discuss that." He had an uneasy feeling about where this conversation was leading.

"You must really be into it," Shorty said.

Tucker nodded in agreement. "Yep, that menu-planning must be absorbing your interest, big-time."

"Not really."

"Must be," Shorty said. "I figure it's on your mind 24/7."

"Of course it's not. That's ridiculous."

Shorty leaned back in his chair with a smile. "I don't know how else to explain the fact that you were moaning and calling out Aurelia's name in the middle of the night."

Not much could make Matthew blush, but he felt his ears getting very warm. "You're making that up."

"No, he's not." Bob picked up his bottle of beer. "I heard you, too. At first I thought you were in pain, but then I realized it was a different kind of pain." His lips twitched. "The pain of true love." He took a drink of his beer.

"Oh, for God's sake." Matthew blew out a breath. "Okay, I find her attractive. I mean, who wouldn't?"

"Hey, we totally understand," Shorty said. "In fact, we're only telling you this because if you're going to keep us awake at night with your moaning and groaning, we'd like to suggest that you just spend the night with Aurelia. With our blessings."

"It worked for Watkins," Danny said. "He got to where he just kept his clothes here but he spent the night up in Mary Lou's apartment. And you're in Watkins' bunk, so why not follow in his footsteps?"

"Yeah, but Watkins ended up married," Matthew said. "This thing between Aurelia and me is temporary. Neither one of us is thinking long-term."

"That's fine. Your business." Shorty pointed his fork at Matthew. "But, that's even more reason to spend the night up there. Make the most of the opportunity."

Matthew picked at the label on his beer bottle. "I've been wondering something. She's a beautiful woman, so how come one of you didn't make a move before I got here?"

"I wouldn't have," Tucker said. "I'm engaged."

"The rest of us talked about it," Bob admitted. "But none of us felt like we could flirt with her and then turn around and complain about her food behind her back. It took somebody like you who actually *likes* her food to make any headway. So we're happy for you."

"And we'll be even happier if we don't have to listen to that lovesick caterwauling we heard last night," Shorty said.

"Sorry about that." Matthew's ears still felt warm, but the guys had done him a favor. Assuming Aurelia would let him stay, he could spend the entire night enjoying her many charms. That was worth a little embarrassment.

As he had the night before, he played cards with the guys until just before eight. They kept getting in digs the entire time, but he didn't care. The only person who could rain on his parade at this point was Aurelia, if she refused to let him occupy her bed.

He didn't expect that, so when he excused himself from the game, he went over and pulled his duffel out from under his bunk so he could stuff several condoms into his pockets. He tried to be subtle about it, but apparently he didn't succeed.

"Be sure you take enough," Shorty called out.

"Yeah, it's hell to run out," Danny added.

The guys were still laughing when he grabbed his hat from the rack by the door and pushed through the screen door. Then he thought of something and turned around.

"What did you forget?" Shorty asked, pulling his cigar out of his mouth as Matthew came back in. "Your sex toys?"

"No. I forgot to warn you bozos that if a single one of you makes an inappropriate remark to Aurelia about any of this, I will personally wipe up the floor with you. You can kid me all you want, but leave her alone."

"We're all good cowboys," Danny said. The laughter had faded from his eyes. "And a good cowboy doesn't insult women. And while we're on the subject of Aurelia, we all think she's a nice person. Weird cooking, but a nice person. Don't break her heart."

"I don't intend to do that," Matthew said quietly. "We're both going into this with our eyes wide open."

Tucker gazed at him, his expression doubtful. "You may be, but take care with her, okay?"

Matthew bristled at the suggestion that he wouldn't, but he tamped down that spurt of anger. They were being protective, and there was nothing wrong with that. He touched the brim of his hat. "Understood. See you boys in the morning."

As he walked up to the house in the apricot glow of a midsummer twilight, with crickets chirping and an owl hooting from the top of a spruce tree, Matthew thought about what Tucker had said. Tucker and Aurelia had spent some time talking this afternoon beside the corral.

Matthew hoped to hell Tucker hadn't told her about him talking in his sleep last night. Or more accurately, *moaning* in his sleep. Dear God, had he really been as pathetic as the guys had made him sound? Probably not. They were laying it on thick because they hadn't been able to resist.

Surely Tucker hadn't said anything to Aurelia. That would be breaking an unspoken code unless you had it in for the guy. Tucker had no reason to sabotage Matthew.

But Tucker had seemed sincere when he'd told Matthew to treat Aurelia well. Maybe he had noticed something in her behavior that indicated she was more vulnerable than Matthew thought. He needed to be alert to any signs that she was getting in over her head, because the last thing he wanted to do was hurt her.

So far, though, she'd seemed to be fine with the rules of the game. More than fine. She'd carried last night's entertainment beyond where he would have. Thinking about it gave him an erection that made walking painful, so he did his best to push it out of his mind.

Pockets bulging slightly with the condoms he'd tucked there, he climbed the steps to the back door and rapped on the screen the way he had the night before. His heart beat a rapid tattoo as he remembered what had happened the last time he'd gone through this door. But if Aurelia was okay with it, they'd have all night to enjoy each other, so no laundry-room sex was called for.

She came to the door with a much louder greeting than she'd given him the previous night. "Matthew! We were just talking about you."

"I hope it was good things." So she wasn't alone in the kitchen. He reined in his disappointment with the thought that he didn't have to go back to the bunk-house tonight. If they couldn't be alone now, they'd be alone later.

"All good things. Sarah and Pete think you're doing a terrific job with Houdini." She drew him inside and squeezed his hand. "Come on in and have a little steak, and then we'll discuss tomorrow's menu."

He took heart from that little squeeze. She was going to be as happy to see Sarah and Pete leave as he was. But it was Sarah's house, and Pete was her fiancé, so they had more right to be here than he did. He just hoped the bulge of extra condoms in his pockets wasn't too noticeable.

As he passed through the laundry room, he took off his hat but kept hold of it instead of tossing it on the dryer. But he'd never be able to look at another clothes dryer again without thinking of having sex with Aurelia on top of it. He didn't dare think about it now, though, when he was about to walk into a brightly lit kitchen and make small talk with the people who had hired him to train their horse.

Sarah and Pete sat at the same small table Aurelia had slipped underneath the night before in order to provide him with a wonderful sensual gift. He'd be better off not thinking about that, either.

Tonight a bassett hound was under the table, his head on his paws. Matthew had heard that Sarah had a dog, but he'd never met the pooch. He said hello to Sarah and Pete before crouching down by the table. "And who's this?" The hound gazed up at Matthew with sad eyes and his tail thumped the floor in greeting, but he seemed content to stay where he was.

"Rodney Dangerfield," Sarah said. "He believes in economy of movement. He's not the sort of dog who races to the door when you come home, or scrambles to his feet to say hello to a visitor, especially after his dinner."

"I see." Matthew held out a hand for the dog to sniff. He got a lick in return. "Nice to meet you, too, Rodney." He scratched behind Rodney's big floppy ears, and the dog sighed in apparent contentment. But he still didn't move. "No, please don't get up. Don't trouble yourself, Rodney, really."

Sarah laughed. "I wanted a tracking dog, and I found Rodney listed in a shelter in Colorado. Pete and I took a drive down there and picked him up."

"He's a good tracker, too," Pete added, "once he gets moving. And if you ever want to wake up the neighborhood, Rodney's your guy."

"I'll keep those things in mind." As Matthew rose to his feet again, he noticed Sarah and Pete each had a glass of wine, but the glasses were nearly empty. Good. He hoped they didn't decide on a refill, although it really wasn't his place to wish something like that. This was Sarah's kitchen, after all.

Pete stood and offered his hand to Matthew. "I wanted to officially thank you. Apparently you've managed to combine training that horse with helping the kids. That's impressive."

Matthew shook Pete's hand. "It wasn't planned, believe me. Lester gets the credit. He finished his work early yesterday so he could come and watch me, and the more I looked at him, the more I thought Houdini might accept the weight of a boy his size. I had no idea Houdini had fond memories of a teenager who'd been nice to him. That was pure luck."

"Well, it's all those kids can talk about, and Lester has become the mascot of the group."

"He has the potential to be a talented trainer when he's a little older."

Sarah nodded enthusiastically. "I so agree. I told Pete we need to keep track of that boy and hire him at the Last Chance once he's of age."

"He'd be an asset." Matthew couldn't help feeling

proud of his part in Lester's blossoming, although as he'd said, it had been partly by accident.

"As for the other boy, Jeff." Pete shook his head. "I didn't do a good enough job vetting him and I apologize for that."

Sarah reached over and squeezed his hand. "Don't blame yourself. Jeff has learned how to charm people when it suits his purpose."

"The boys were asking this afternoon if Jeff will come back," Aurelia said. "Tucker mentioned that the Last Chance doesn't give up on people or animals, and they wanted to know if you'd given up on Jeff. Tucker said something about counseling."

"That's right," Pete said. "I've set him up with a top-notch counselor and talked with his foster parents. I'm going to monitor his progress for the next few months and see if we can give him another shot next summer, but he'd be here on probation if that even happens. One screw-up and he'd be gone for good."

Matthew was reassured that Pete wouldn't turn Jeff loose on the Last Chance community anytime soon. "He needs to get his act together before he's allowed near the animals."

"I agree." Still standing, Pete picked up his wineglass and drained it. "Ready to call it a night, my love?"

"Yes." Sarah drank the rest of her wine. "Now that the boys are all settled upstairs with their books and their video games, I'm ready to turn in."

Matthew kept his expression neutral. He hadn't realized that Pete sometimes stayed overnight with Sarah, but, just as with him and Aurelia, that was their business.

Sarah peered under the table. "Come on, Rodney. Time to drag yourself down the hall, big boy."

The dog took his time getting to his feet, but once he did, he followed Sarah and Pete as they started out of the kitchen. "Good night, you two," Sarah said over her shoulder. "Don't stay up too late planning tomorrow's menus."

"We won't," Aurelia said. "Good night." After giving them ample time to walk down the hall and continue on to Sarah's bedroom, she turned to Matthew. "Ready for a little steak?"

"Among other things." He drew her into his arms. "The guys kicked me out of the bunkhouse."

Her eyes widened. "Why?"

He pulled her in closer and relished the feel of her body tucked against his and her arms wrapped around his neck. "They seemed to think I should be up here with you, instead."

Her expression grew speculative. "They know something's going on, don't they? I could tell when I talked to Tucker."

"Why? What did he say?" Matthew mentally crossed his fingers that no discussion of moaning had taken place.

"He just found it interesting that you took over Watkins's bunk, and Watkins got involved with the cook. I think he sees history repeating itself."

"Up to a point."

"Right." Her gaze was steady. "Up to a point."

"So I can stay?"

"Did you bring more than one condom?"

"I did."

She smiled and moved her hips suggestively against the bulge in his jeans. "Then yes, you can stay, cowboy."

9

"HERE'S MY IDEA, now that I know I have you for the whole night." Aurelia couldn't believe her good fortune. She'd expected Matthew to say he had to leave in an hour or so. "Let's do the menu-planning first and be done with it."

"That's a sensible idea." He pulled her in tighter. "But I don't feel like being sensible. I want to kiss you." He lowered his head.

"No." She wiggled out of his embrace. "I know what happens once you start kissing me." She hurried over to a cupboard and pulled out a stack of cookbooks. "Here." She shoved them at his chest. "Take these to the table."

He laughed, but he accepted the cookbooks and laid his hat on the table. "Bossy little thing, aren't you?"

"Wouldn't you rather have this out of the way so we can concentrate on…each other?" She glanced deliberately at his crotch.

He drew in a sharp breath. "You do know how to win an argument. I've been thinking about that under-the-table maneuver all day."

"Liar. You've been training Houdini most of the day."

"When I wasn't training Houdini I was thinking of it." He sat down and flipped open the first cookbook. "When do I get my steak? It smells wonderful."

"I'm keeping it warm in the oven and I'll give it to you once we retire to my bedroom."

He glanced up, his gaze hot. "That sounded almost as if you plan to feed it to me."

"I might, at that." She noticed the cookbook he was paging through. "Forget about that one for now. The second one in the stack has the recipe I was considering. It's on page fifty-two."

He put aside the first book and thumbed through the second until he came to the recipe. "Beef with carrots? Seriously?"

"You don't think they'll like it?"

"They'll love it, but I can't believe you'd pick something so…basic."

"Reverse psychology." She sat across the table from him. "It's only beef and carrots with some spices, but I'm going to tell them it's *Boeuf avec carottes* and stick in some sprigs of thyme to make it look more exotic. I want them to realize that just because something has a French name doesn't mean they won't like it."

"Brilliant. So are we done? Can we put these away, now?"

"I want to make stuffed turnips for dinner."

"Oh." He shook his head. "I don't think that will work."

"It might, and I'm willing to take a chance. They're getting Mary Lou's chocolate chip cookies for lunch, and her chocolate pie for dinner, so I think it's time to add something different, like stuffed turnips."

"What are they stuffed with? Because if it's goat cheese, I've heard about the goat cheese, and it's not popular. The guys have a real problem with goat cheese, and I—"

"Matthew, Matthew." She walked over and cupped his face in both hands. "Chill. It'll be fine. There's no goat cheese."

He caught her hand and turned his head so he could place a lingering, erotic kiss on her palm. "Thank you."

Just that one kiss, which didn't even land on her mouth, and she was consumed with lust. But she tried her best to sound breezy and nonchalant, as if he hadn't turned her into mush with one touch of his lips. If she intended to convince herself that she could handle this affair without getting sentimental, she had to master breezy and nonchalant.

"You seemed a little frantic regarding the goat cheese," she said.

"Maybe it's because they know we're involved, so I'm afraid they'll be watching for me to take a dive."

That made her laugh. "Take a dive? You mean like let me make something outrageous because you're sleeping with me and now have a conflict of interest?"

He gazed up at her. "Yeah, something like that."

"I won't do that to you, Matthew. The stuffed turnips are a little bit different, but not gag-me different. I'll try to come up with something else to put with it that they'll like."

"I don't suppose you'd consider hot dogs."

"No, but..." She had an inspiration. "Forget the stuffed turnips. I'll make pizza and put everything from the turnip recipe on the pizza."

"Turnip pizza? I don't think that's a very good—"

"Trust me, Matthew. I'm starting to get the hang of the menu wars. It's not so much what you do as how you sell it."

He smiled. "That could be said for a lot of things."

"I guess so."

Reaching up, he stroked his knuckles over her throat and down to the V of her purple sleeveless blouse. "Like this button you left undone, for instance. It makes a guy think that when one button is unfastened, why not two?" He demonstrated his skill at that activity by slipping the second button free while still holding her gaze.

She wouldn't have thought such big hands would be so adept at delicate tasks. Thinking of what else those hands could accomplish made her pulse skitter. "I suppose it could have that effect."

"Just so you know, whatever you're selling, I'm buying." Still looking into her eyes, he undid another button.

"But you haven't even inspected the goods."

"Yes, but I intend to." He slipped another button free and glanced down at the purple lace he'd uncovered. "Mmm. Very pretty."

"Glad you like it." She quivered with anticipation.

"Oh, and the bra's nice, too." Leaning forward, he pressed his mouth against the spot just above her cleavage.

It was their only point of contact, and yet his moist, velvet touch sent waves of delight to the tips of her fingers and toes, and straight up to the roots of her hair. She closed her eyes as he made a slow circle with his tongue and blew on it.

"That's *O* for orgasm," he murmured. "I owe you one."

If he continued this subtle but effective assault, they'd soon be even. Her panties were already wet. "Are we keeping score?"

"That wouldn't be fair." Glancing up at her, he slowly redid the buttons, including the one she'd left open on purpose because it gave a shadowy glimpse of cleavage. He'd been right about her motivation on that. "Given half a chance, I can rack up points faster than you can."

"You think so, do you?" Her body tightened, wanting him to prove it ASAP.

"After last night, I know so."

"Them's bold words, cowboy."

"I'll bet a pocketful of condoms on it."

She took a shaky breath. "The way you're talking, you may not want to bother with that steak I have warming in the oven."

He adopted a drawl. "Oh, yes, I do, little lady. It smells absolutely delicious, and I'm looking forward to having you serve me dinner in bed."

Her eyebrows rose. "I see. But in order for me to do that, you'd have to actually be in a bed." She could hardly wait to have this big muscular cowboy stretched out naked on a mattress.

"That's true. Do you happen to have one handy?"

She stepped back and pointed. "Right through that door." She'd put on clean sheets, folded them back and dimmed the lights. "I'll bring your tray in shortly."

"Excellent." He stood and cupped the back of her head. "I'll look forward to it." Then he kissed her with enough tongue, heat and passion to leave her gasping as he walked through the door and into her bedroom. "Don't forget I like it juicy and hot," he called over his shoulder.

"Not a problem." Both she and the steak would satisfy that requirement nicely.

MATTHEW STARTED STRIPPING off his clothes the minute he stepped inside the room. Aurelia kept a neat bedroom, which didn't surprise him, so he folded his clothes and laid them on a suede-covered easy chair in the corner by the window. The curtains were drawn, but two bedside table lamps, their bases made of carved wooden stirrups, cast a muted glow through shades created to look like leather.

Although Matthew had been perfectly happy sleeping in the bunkhouse, he'd be even happier sleeping—or not sleeping—in this little room. The comforter on the queen bed had a cattle-brand pattern and was turned down to reveal smooth white sheets. He hoped they wouldn't be smooth for long.

As he undressed, he took stock of the Charles Remington paintings on the wall, the wagon-wheel headboard and the braided rugs on either side of the bed. The room had been decorated in Old West nostalgia, and Matthew loved it. As much as he enjoyed being on the move, there was something to be said for staying put long enough to create a personally pleasing room like this one.

She had an attached bath, which meant they were self-contained in this apartment off the kitchen. The setup felt cozy and sexy as hell. They could have some good times in this room while he was at the Last Chance.

Tucking a condom behind the lamp on the bedside table, he propped a couple of pillows against the headboard and climbed into bed. He pulled the sheet up and had to laugh at the tent effect. But he didn't want her to laugh, too, so he added the comforter.

"Hot and juicy, coming up." She walked through the door carrying a lap tray fragrant with the scent of roast beef. A glass of red wine sat on the tray, along with a slice of what he'd bet was homemade bread. But it wasn't the food that made his mouth water.

In the midst of preparing his tray, she'd managed to reconfigure her outfit. She was minus the bra, and she'd left the blouse unbuttoned but tied at her midriff. Technically her breasts were covered, but not by much. Her jeans were gone, too, leaving only a purple thong between him and paradise. Her feet were bare.

He gulped. "You certainly know how to serve a guy dinner, Aurelia Imogene Smith."

She turned and nudged the door closed with her shoulder before walking over to the bed. "You can pretend you're in a private gentleman's club."

"No pretending necessary. I am." When she leaned over to set the tray on his lap, he got an eyeful, which had a predictable effect.

"Matthew, I can't get the tray to sit straight. Something's…" She started to laugh. "Something's in the way. I wonder what it could be?"

"Yeah, I wonder. You walk in here looking like a *Playboy* centerfold and then you want to set a bed tray down on my lap. That tray's little legs aren't high enough to accommodate the issue, Aurelia."

She was laughing so hard she was threatening to spill the entire tray, juicy steak and all, onto the bed. He took it from her. "Let me handle this." He set it next to him, making sure that it was steady before he let go. Then he climbed out of bed, erection and all. "You see what we're dealing with here."

Tears ran down her rosy cheeks. "Yes," she said, gasping for breath. "And I have to admit I didn't factor that into this dinner-in-bed concept. I just thought I'd give you a little thrill along with your meal."

"Turns out it was a really big thrill."

"I can see that." She glanced at his rigid penis and clutched her sides in helpless laughter. "Maybe if we set some books under the legs of the tray, it won't wobble and you can…" But she couldn't finish the sentence because she was doubled over with the hilarity of it all.

He saw the humor in the situation, but it was his pride and joy giving her hysterics, and he'd rather have the woman he was with be struck with reverence and awe than practically rolling on the floor at the sight of… And that's when he decided what to do.

Reaching behind the lamp, he located the condom and put it on.

She noticed, which was a step in the right direction. "Matthew?"

"I thought we'd be doing this on the bed next time." With one arm around her shoulders and the other behind her knees, he scooped her up easily and laid her down on the braided rug. "But apparently not."

She still had the giggles. "The floor? With a bed

right there, you're going to—" Her eyes widened as he stripped away her thong in one quick movement. "I guess you are."

"Yes, ma'am." His first thrust lifted her off the rug, but then he settled into a more gentle rhythm. And after that first protest, she didn't seem to mind a bit that they were flat on the floor.

In fact, she got into it, wrapping her legs around his waist and rising to meet him with each stroke. Arms braced on either side of her shoulders, he gazed down at her, entranced by finally being able to look into her green eyes as they turned dark with excitement.

Her skin blushed pink, and their wild movements had set her breasts free of the blouse. They spilled out in all their glory, her nipples wine-red and tight with passion. Slowing his pace even more, he leaned down and closed his mouth over one tempting nub.

As he sucked rhythmically, he felt her first spasm roll over his cock. Restraining his own orgasm, he kept his mouth at her breast as he stroked deeper, coaxing her higher and higher yet. At last he nipped lightly at her breast and she came in a rush, her body arching off the rug and quivering beneath him.

Releasing her nipple, he shifted his angle and pumped faster. "One more." His vocal cords felt like sandpaper. "Do that again."

Her surrender was beautiful to watch. She abandoned her inhibitions and begged him to go faster as she clutched his hips. She writhed beneath him, thrashing her head from side to side, reaching for that next explosion, and when he gave it to her, he came, too, burying himself in her pulsing center as he murmured her name over and over, and over again.

They lay on the rug, limp and spent, for a very long time. The thought drifted through his mind that maybe Aurelia wasn't the only one at risk for a broken heart. It was a soft warning, not an urgent one, and he chose to push it aside. This was good, very good, but he could learn to live without it. Of course he could.

At last he propped himself up on his elbow and started fiddling with the knot she'd made in order to hold her blouse together. She lay beneath him, eyes closed and arms flung out to her sides, while he labored over the knot. He wanted the blouse gone. He craved seeing Aurelia naked in the soft glow of the bedside lamps.

She stirred, although her eyes remained closed. But her full mouth tilted in a smile. "There's an easier way."

"I've almost got it."

"If I lift my arms up, you can pull it over my head."

It was a testament to his lust-soaked brain that he hadn't thought of that. "Then please lift your arms up, because I want you naked and totally accessible."

As she raised her arms over her head, her eyes opened slowly, revealing banked fires. "And why, exactly, do you need me to be totally accessible?"

"So I can inspect the goods." He worked the blouse upward, but it took a while, because he had to keep stopping to kiss her warm skin along the way. She was a marvel, a delicacy, a feast the likes of which he hadn't experienced in his quest for lean, tough, undomesticated women. Aurelia was so incredibly soft.

"You do realize your steak is getting cold."

He'd forgotten completely about the steak, which he'd made a big deal out of earlier, and she'd taken great pains to warm it and serve it to him. True, she'd sabotaged the effort by showing up looking like a wet dream, but she hadn't factored in the logistics.

The bottom line was that he needed to eat that steak. He finally divested her of the blouse, which meant she was as accessible as he could ever want. The sight of her lying there in the lamplight caused his cock to stir restlessly again.

But if he didn't eat the steak and give the food the attention it deserved, she might be insulted, and an insulted lover wasn't a happy lover. He'd eaten in enough high-end restaurants to know that cooks were a temperamental lot.

He'd have to make sure that she knew he was crazy about what she'd fixed for him. In order to do that, he'd have to use all his powers of concentration so that he wouldn't abandon the food in favor of the woman.

"Tell you what," he said. "I need to take care of a little chore connected to the fun we just had. When I get back from the bathroom, that tray should fit over my lap at least long enough for me to enjoy the steak you saved for me. I really do want it."

She met his gaze. "It's still juicy, but it won't be hot."

He gave her a long, slow kiss before easing away from her. "I'm sure it will be absolutely wonderful. I can hardly wait."

10

AURELIA TREATED HERSELF to the view of Matthew's tight buns as he walked into the bathroom. Then she picked up the thong he'd stripped off and the blouse he'd pulled over her head. Her body hummed with lingering vibrations from two spectacular climaxes. As a woman, she reveled in the pleasure he'd given her, but as a chef, she fretted that his steak would no longer be the optimal temperature.

It was a challenge pleasing a man sexually and gastronomically when he wanted both pleasures delivered at approximately the same time. From now on she would make an effort to space them further apart. That might be tricky to do, though, when they were so hungry for each other.

When he walked back into the bedroom, she forgot her worries about the temperature of the steak. Seeing Matthew Tredway naked would wipe all logical thought out of any woman's mind. His wide shoulders and broad chest represented a solid strength that a man like Matthew would use to defend the weak and the vulnerable. She was neither, but admired him for it, nevertheless.

He glanced at the tray perched on the bed. "That wine will go great with the steak, but—"

"That's right. You don't like to drink alone."

"Not if there's an alternative."

She opened her closet door and grabbed a white cotton bathrobe. "I'll be right back with another glass." She didn't think walking naked through the kitchen was a good idea, even if everyone was supposed to be tucked in for the night.

"Bring the bottle," he called out after her.

She smiled to herself. If anyone happened to be within earshot of that remark, they'd know immediately what was going on in the cook's apartment. Aurelia thought Sarah and Pete knew, anyway. But she didn't want any of the teenagers to figure it out.

Fortunately the kitchen was empty and the house was quiet. She could just barely hear a hip-hop number that was probably coming from an iPod speaker upstairs, but the house was so big and the walls so thick that it seemed very far away.

She'd loved that about the ranch house from her first day here. Her apartment building back home in Nebraska allowed her to hear far more of her neighbors' activities than she cared to. She was saving for a house of her own, but she didn't have a down payment that satisfied her yet.

She wondered if Matthew had some sort of residence or if he lived out of a post office box. She decided to ask him, because it seemed like the sort of thing she should know about a man she was sleeping with.

Armed with the bottle and a second glass, she returned to the bedroom and found Matthew back in bed with the tray balanced perfectly on his lap.

He glanced up with a smile. "See? It works fine."

"It does, at that." She walked over to the other side of the bed and set the wine and her glass on the lamp table. Then she started to slip off her bathrobe.

"Maybe you should keep that on for now."

"Okay." She laughed. "Want me to sit over in the chair, out of reach?"

"Might be a good idea. My clothes are on it. Sorry about that."

"I can move them." She transferred his clothes to the end of the bed, picked up her wineglass and returned to the suede-covered easy chair. The chair had never seemed particularly erotic before, but now the material rubbed sensuously against her bare calves as she sat down.

To be fair, she'd never sat and watched a naked man lounging against a bank of snowy white pillows while he ate something she'd cooked. She'd thought staying across the room from him would lessen the temptation for her, too. Not so much.

From this vantage point she could watch his muscles flex when he raised the fork. She was super-conscious of his mouth, the square line of his jaw and the tanned column of his throat. She became fascinated by the gentle rise and fall of his chest and the pattern of the dark hair that lightly covered his strong pecs and then arrowed downward.

"This is terrific." He took small bites, not wolfing it down the way some men might have. "I would have hated to miss it."

"Then I'm glad I saved you some." She couldn't deny that his praise felt really good. She cooked to explore her creative side, but knowing that someone savored the result of her efforts made the experience really shine for her.

Still, the longer she watched him, the more she ached for his touch. Sipping her wine, she tried to control her impatience. She wanted him to take his time and enjoy the food she'd prepared. Of course she did. But right now she had competing needs, and sexuality was winning out.

She'd lost interest in her wine and set the glass on the floor beside her chair in hopes that would be a subtle signal for him to hurry up. He didn't seem to notice, so she casually loosened the tie of her bathrobe so the lapels would gape a little.

"It's amazing that you could warm this up without making it dry." Without so much as a glance in her direction, he speared another small piece of steak. "But it's really tasty."

So am I, so can we move on? "Thank you." She took a long, slow breath, which caused the bathrobe to shift, revealing even more if he should happen to glance over.

Instead he seemed completely focused on his food. She hadn't given him much. She couldn't see what was left on his plate, but surely he was almost finished.

"Have you ever thought of turning pro?"

Her brain was on sex, so the question startled her. Then she recalibrated. He was talking about becoming a professional *chef.* "No, not really. This gig is more like an expansion of cooking for friends and family, but I don't crave a job in a restaurant. Too impersonal."

He continued to pay great attention to his plate. "I can understand that, but you're very talented."

I have talents in other areas, too. Let's explore those, shall we? She decided subtle wasn't working. She slipped her arms out of the bathrobe and picked up her wine.

"I wish there was a way for you to have a wider audience."

She stood, but still he didn't notice. She dipped her finger in the wine.

"I wish—"

She interrupted him with a deliberate clearing of her throat.

He looked up then, and his fork, along with a tiny bite of steak, clattered back onto the plate.

Slowly she circled her nipple with one moist finger. Then she slipped her finger into the wine again and repeated the process on the other side. Wetting her finger once more, she drew a line from her breasts down to an area she knew would grab his attention.

As her finger disappeared in a mass of curls, the lap tray rattled. Snapping out of his trance, Matthew moved it quickly to the floor, threw back the covers and climbed out of bed, revealing in the process why the tray had jiggled.

Holding her gaze, he walked over and took the wineglass from her unresisting fingers. "Allow me."

"Happy to."

Swirling his finger in her wine, he slowly painted her mouth. "Bored, were we?" He followed the path of his finger with his tongue.

"Uh-huh." But not now. Anticipation fizzed in her veins.

Tucking back her hair, he used his wine-wet finger to trace the curve of her ear. "I wanted you to know..." he paused to slowly lick away the wine, sending shivers through her "...how much I love your food."

"I figured." Her breath caught as he flicked a droplet of wine into the hollow of her throat and sucked it away.

"Apparently I overdid it." He trailed a damp finger over her collarbone, followed by the smooth slide of his tongue.

"A little."

"I'll make it up to you." He circled her nipple, anointing it as she had done, before leaning down and drawing it into his mouth.

She felt the tug all the way down to her womb and clutched his broad shoulders for support. "I'm sure..." As he rolled her nipple between his tongue and the roof of his mouth, she forgot what else she'd meant to say.

Splaying his big hand at the small of her back, he steadied her as he made sweet love to her breast with his hot, hungry mouth. His cheeks hollowed and his talented tongue brought her the kind of pleasure she'd been so impatient for.

Moaning, she cupped the back of his head with both hands and tunneled her fingers into his thick hair. Her breathing grew shallow and her pulse urgent as he transferred his attention to her other breast. He rubbed it with wine and licked it clean before centering on her aching nipple.

"I think you're going to come for me," he murmured against her skin. "I think you're ready."

"Mmm." Her eyes drifted shut as he closed his mouth over her breast and began driving her slowly insane. Her body tightened, reaching for release.

His teeth raked her nipple, sending a jolt of sensation straight to her trigger point. He sucked in again, resuming the rhythmic beat that took her closer, and closer yet.

Still holding the wineglass, he brushed his knuckles over her quivering body, heading down, down, before stopping at the critical point. As his teeth caught her nipple again, he pressed his knuckle in right *there*. Shoving her fist against her mouth to muffle her cries, she came apart.

The room seemed to whirl around her. It was a testament to his strength that he could hold a wineglass and turn her around without spilling a drop.

"Down you go."

Still dazed from her orgasm, she offered no resistance as he guided her to a sitting position on the edge of the bed. When he told her to lie back, she did that, too. And then, when she felt the slow drip of what must have been wine, and his tongue caressing a part of her that continued to quiver from his last campaign, she understood.

He'd said he'd make it up to her, and obviously he wasn't even close to being finished. And as he settled in, she decided that of all the things she admired about Matthew Tredway, this might turn out to be her favorite.

Ah, he was good. No, excellent. No, world-class… And then her brain ceased to function as sensation took over, carrying her on a hot river of lust that kept widening and churning as it headed for a thundering drop. She went over the edge gladly, and this time she didn't remember to muffle her cries. Sometimes a girl just had to jump in a barrel and go over the falls.

As she lay gulping for air, her arms flung out to her sides, he kissed his way back up her body. She opened her eyes to his smiling, very triumphant, expression.

"Am I forgiven for boring you?"

She managed to nod, which was about all the response she was capable of making at the moment.

"Good, because I have a little problem. Wait, that's false modesty. I have a really *big* problem, and I need your help with it, if you'd be willing to scoot up onto the bed…there, that's fine, and…just a second, I have to suit up…there."

She took a shaky breath. "I don't know if I have any more orgasms left."

"Maybe not. You can just lie still if you want." He moved over her. "I don't mind. I just need to…ah." He thrust in deep. "You are so wet."

"Your fault."

Braced on his forearms, he gazed down at her as he began to slowly pump. "I'll take the blame. Is this okay? I don't want to overstay my welcome."

"It's okay." Gradually, it was becoming several notches above okay. She'd thought he'd exhausted the possibilities for her with that double whammy moments ago, but now, as his steady thrusts reached remembered spots of delight, she found herself rising to meet his strokes.

His eyebrows lifted. "You don't have to do that, you know."

"I know." She clutched his firm buns. "Turns out I might have another orgasm hiding in there, after all."

"Nice to know." His blue eyes darkened as he shifted his angle. "That makes this a lot more fun."

Her pulse hammered as the increased friction built the tension even faster. "I like that angle."

"Thought you might." His words were husky and laced with urgency.

His excitement fueled her own. "Oh, yeah. Mmm, good." She'd never reacted this way with a man in her life, but Matthew brought out the wild woman in her. Sliding her hands up his back, she felt his powerful muscles tremble beneath her palms.

She loved having him deep inside her, as close as they could get. Longing to be even closer, she lifted her legs and wrapped them around his waist.

He sucked in a breath. "Nice."

"You like?"

"I do." His groan of happiness was followed by a faster pace and the erotic slap of his balls against her thighs. "But it's too good. I can't…"

"It's…okay. I'm…*there*." Her climax arrived to the sound of Matthew's bellow of satisfaction. Waves of sensation rolled through her as her spasms blended with his. His big body shuddered in the aftermath, and she held him tight, relishing how their combined shock waves extended the pleasure. She wouldn't have been surprised if they were giving off sparks.

After their bodies finally stopped shaking, Matthew looked into her eyes. "That was seriously good."

She took a deep breath. "I'd have to agree."

"The dryer and the rug were okay for novelty's sake, but I have to say, there's a reason most people have sex in bed."

"So they can go to sleep afterward?"

He smiled. "That, too. I'm looking forward to going to sleep cuddled up with you, Aurelia." He extracted himself from her tight embrace. "Be right back."

She was looking forward to sleeping in his arms, too—maybe a little too much. He'd left the bathroom door open, so she called out to him. "Matthew, do you live somewhere?"

"I live everywhere. Why?"

"I mean, do you have a place that you go back to when you're not traveling?"

"I have an apartment in Dallas, but I don't spend much time there. Sometimes I wonder if the apartment's necessary, although I'd need somewhere to store my extra clothes. I suppose my real home is on my website on the internet. That's where customers find me. But I do have this little apartment in Dallas."

"Why there?"

"It's a major hub for the airlines, and you can pick up international flights out of there. Plus the flying weather is usually decent."

"So you don't have any ties there, then? Family?"

"I have friends in Dallas." He walked out of the bathroom looking his usual manly self. "But then I have friends in a lot of places." Climbing into bed, he gathered her close.

She noticed he hadn't responded to the question about family, but she'd leave that for now. She laid her cheek on his chest as if she'd been doing it for years. He was so easy to be with. "And now you have a friend in Nebraska."

"I sure hope so." He kissed the top of her head.

"Of course, one of these days you'll marry some great guy, so our friendship will have to change and become strictly platonic, but I'd like to think we could still be in touch."

Being platonic friends with Matthew was a very depressing thought. "Or you could end up getting married."

"Not likely."

"Are you sure?" She listened to the steady beat of his heart. It was such a loving heart that she found it impossible to imagine he'd be satisfied with temporary affairs forever.

"I don't see how I can ask a woman to make that kind of sacrifice." He stroked her hair. "I love my work, and I love the places it takes me. I can't ask anyone to trail along after me trying to piece together a life that fits with mine."

"What if she's into horses, like you are?" Why she was trying to hook him up with someone was a mystery, except that his plan seemed so…lonely.

"She'd have to be committed to helping problem horses, love to travel, and be willing to abandon the idea of a home and kids. Oh, and we'd have to be wildly attracted to each other. That's not an easy person to find."

"I suppose not." She snuggled closer. "But you deserve someone, Matthew, someone wonderful."

"At this very moment, I have someone wonderful right here."

"I mean full-time, for the long run."

He chuckled. "Ready to hit the road with me, Aurelia?"

"I'd be a terrible choice. I'm not a traveler at all."

"You said that when we first met, and I'm still not all that clear on why."

She shrugged. "I come from a long line of non-travelers. We're all perfectly happy to stay close to home. It's amazing that my Aunt Mary Lou came as far as Jackson Hole."

"Hmm." Matthew rubbed her back. "So what's your aunt doing off on a cruise through the Panama Canal, then?"

"Her new husband talked her into it, I guess, but I predict she'll hate it."

"Well, even if she does, I owe her a lot for taking a honeymoon cruise that required a replacement cook, and I'm very glad you were willing to leave the state of Nebraska for three weeks to fill in here."

"Me, too." When she'd arrived, three weeks had seemed like a long time. Not anymore, especially now that she'd started this affair with Matthew. "How much longer are you planning to stay at the Last Chance?"

He laughed softly. "I like that question. It sounds like you want me to stick around awhile."

"That's because I do."

"The Chance family paid me a flat fee plus room and board, which is the only fair way for me to do my job, because I never know how much time the training will take."

She thought about the progress he'd made already. "You seem to be moving right along with Houdini."

"He's doing very well. I'd say I'm ahead of schedule with him."

Her stomach tightened. "So you might leave soon?"

"It's possible I could finish up in another three or

four days, but I have a feeling this project will take me longer than that. I want to make sure I do a thorough job."

The knot in her tummy loosened. "It's probably better for Houdini if you take your time."

He rolled her to her back. "I'm not talking about training Houdini." He nuzzled her throat. "I'm talking about loving you."

11

MATTHEW FELL EASILY into a routine of working with Houdini and the kids during the day and spending every night with Aurelia. He couldn't seem to get enough of her ripe body. Climbing into bed with her, he dropped ten years and became a sex-mad twenty-something again.

Her enthusiasm had lots to do with it. She made no attempt to hide the fact that she'd never had sex this good before and wanted to take advantage of their brief time together. He felt the same way. If sex had ever been this good for him, he couldn't remember when.

He'd also admitted to himself that having her cook for him was a turn-on. Maybe she didn't cook specifically for him, but because he helped her plan the menus, he felt as if she prepared everything with him in mind. A curvy woman who provided great sex and great food touched some deep need that he hadn't realized he had.

And finally, he liked hanging out with her in the kitchen and the bedroom while they play-acted a domesticity he never expected to have on a regular basis. He'd given up pretending to live in the bunkhouse while he was here. The cowhands had encouraged him to move his stuff to Aurelia's bedroom and take advantage of a good situation.

But he still hung out at the bunkhouse for a couple of hours around dinner time so he could eat with the guys and play a few hands of poker. He'd taken his turn at cooking and found himself in Aurelia's shoes when he realized how much he wanted the cowhands to like the goulash he'd made. He needed to give her more credit for her courage.

He liked being with the cowhands, plus it meant he wasn't at the main house for dinner with the kids. They hadn't said anything, but being smart and observant, they had to know what was going on. They were good kids, but they wouldn't be able to resist sly looks and winks if he came to dinner every night. He'd rather avoid that, both for Aurelia's sake and his.

He'd taken his duffel full of clothes to Aurelia's room, though, and his laptop. He'd fallen into the habit of sitting in the suede easy chair to answer emails right after lunch. Better then than at night, when he'd rather be doing other things, but he couldn't let his business go to hell in a handbasket.

During one of his sessions on the laptop, he checked out a blog link a friend had sent him. A horse trainer had decided blogging was a good way to advertise his services, and Matthew realized it wasn't a bad idea. He wasn't sure if he had the time or patience, but he'd give it some thought.

Aurelia came into the bedroom just as he was ready to close down the computer. He had to be careful when they were alone during the day, because she tempted him, and they both had work to do. His discipline was tested constantly, but so far he'd kept his life at the ranch compartmentalized.

He glanced up, smiling because he couldn't help it whenever he saw her. The day was warm and she'd worn her hair on top of her head. That, plus her white sleeveless blouse and beige slacks, made her look like summer. He had a sudden image of hot, sweaty sex, but that was a normal mental picture whenever she was around.

He controlled himself. "Lunch was great. They took to that spinach soufflé better than I expected they would."

"Thanks to you, teaching me to prep them first so they wouldn't take one look and think baked frog. Did you get all your emails answered?"

"I did. A friend thinks I should start blogging about horse-training."

Her green eyes lit up. "That's a wonderful idea! I read cooking blogs when I'm at home, and I miss doing that, but I decided not to bring a laptop and I don't want to borrow Sarah's."

He held his out. "Feel free to use mine whenever you want. It's the least I can do."

That made her laugh. She looked so pretty when she laughed that it caused a curious tightness in his chest. He wasn't sure how he was going to survive without that laugh at the end of next week, when they'd both leave the ranch.

"If you're worried about earning your keep, don't be," she said. "I've been more than compensated for sharing my living quarters with you."

"I hope so, because I've…I've really liked being here."

"You're a considerate guest. Your parents must have—" She paused, her cheeks turning pink. "I'm sorry. I promised myself I wouldn't pry into your family background. Sarah says you never talk about it." She looked more uncomfortable than he'd ever seen her. "Sorry."

"Hey." Setting the laptop aside, he stood and took her by the shoulders. "It's a natural comment to make. Don't feel bad about it."

"But I didn't mean—"

"Here's the digest version. My mother died when I was seven and my father passed away a few years ago, still brokenhearted over my mom. I'm one of those people who literally has no family connections, so that's why I don't talk about it. Nothing to say."

She gazed up at him, her eyes full of sympathy.

"Don't look at me like that, Aurelia. I'm fine. We usually don't get all the goodies in life, and I have work that I love. That's more than many can say."

She nodded. "You're right. But thanks for telling me about your folks. I won't spread it around."

"I know you won't. It wouldn't really matter if you did, except sometimes people think they should feel sorry for me, and they shouldn't. I'm a lucky man." He massaged her shoulders. "And now I'd better get down to the barn before I end up kissing you."

"Yeah." She smiled. "We both know we can't stop with just one."

"I'm going to test that." He allowed himself one fast and furious kiss that tasted like heaven. Because he was no angel, he quickly left the bedroom without looking back. It was the only way he could control his lust for the potent combination of sweet and sexy that was Aurelia Imogene Smith.

On the way out, he raised his fist in victory so that she could see, and her laughter followed him. Yeah, he was going to miss that like crazy.

THE CALENDAR BECAME Aurelia's enemy. A large one hung on the kitchen wall and it was quite attractive with its pictures of registered Paint horses. She ignored it as best she could.

When she was in Matthew's arms, thoughts of the calendar would disappear for hours. But then he'd leave in the morning to work with Houdini, and she'd catch a glimpse of that damned wall calendar in the kitchen and realize how few days of paradise remained. Every night they seemed so close, as if nothing could separate them. But the calendar would wrench them apart eventually, and she hated it with a passion.

When they only had six days left, Matthew arrived at his usual time after dinner in a jubilant mood. He always looked really glad to see her, but tonight as she set him up at the table with the fondue she'd served for dinner, he kept grinning at her as if he had a Christmas present in his pocket.

"What's with you?" she asked as she placed a bowl of cut veggies and another one of cubed beef in front of him. "You look like you won the lottery."

"I figured out how you can reach a wider audience with your cooking skills."

She narrowed her eyes. "If you want me to try out

for some cooking competition, you can forget that right now. That's not me."

"I know that. But what I came up with is perfect for you. You're pretty and personable, so you could—"

"Cook in front of an audience? Not on your life!" She brought two glasses and a bottle of wine to the table and sat across from him.

"I wouldn't ask you to do that, either. But what do you say to writing a cooking blog?"

At first she automatically rejected the idea. "No, I don't think…" But before she completed the sentence, she paused, and now she was thinking about it. Anybody could start a blog, which meant that *she* could, too. If nobody read it, then she could just stop. The risk was minimal, the potential fun great.

If people started reading her blog the way she read others, she could share her cooking experiences and learn from those who came to chat. And best of all, she wouldn't have to go anywhere to do it. All she needed was her laptop and a little help from a techie friend to create the site.

Matthew looked pleased with himself. "You're thinking about it, aren't you?" He poured them each some wine.

"Maybe."

"You are. I can tell from the sparkle in those beautiful green eyes. There are all sorts of things going on in your noggin."

"Okay, yes. The more I think about it, the more I like it. It's…" She smiled at him. "Brilliant, Matthew. Pure genius. Will you read it?"

He laughed and raised his glass in a toast. "I'll read yours if you'll read mine."

"You're going to blog?" What a happy little thought. After he left, he'd only be a mouse click away. Sure, it wouldn't be the same, but they'd have a connection and she'd be able to keep up with his travels. Whenever he was nearby, she could invite him for the weekend.

"I decided it couldn't hurt." Using a long-handled fork, he put some veggies in the hot broth. "And while I was thinking how I'd set it up, I got the brainstorm that you could do the same thing with cooking."

"Yours will be a hit. Your readers of *Think Like a Horse* will flock to it." Although she hadn't told him, she'd ordered the book. Sarah had loaned her a copy until it arrived, and she'd managed to snatch moments here and there to read a few pages.

"We'll see." He pulled chunks of carrots and zucchini out of the broth and started cooking the cubed beef. "I'm thinking of writing another book aimed at kids. I could promote that, too."

"Another brilliant idea." In her admittedly prejudiced opinion, he'd write a great book for kids. His positive attitude toward animals, people and life in general shone through his first book, and one aimed at kids likely would have the same can-do spirit.

"I can thank Lester for that project," he said as he began to eat. "I hadn't really planned to work the teenagers into Houdini's training, but Lester showed up and suddenly it seemed like the most logical thing in the world."

"You realize that Lester thinks you're a rock star."

Matthew paused, his fork halfway to his mouth. "He'll get over it."

"I don't think so." She was dangerously close to feeling the same way about Matthew.

"I admire Lester, too, and I've told him so. All the kids are pretty amazing considering the obstacles they've faced in life."

"Very true."

"They've also taught me a lot." He paused to sip some wine. "They react differently to the horses than most adults do. They have fewer preconceived ideas about how to work with them and they're…I don't know…unselfconscious, I guess." He pointed to the fondue pot. "This is really good, by the way."

"Thank you. Would you tell me if it wasn't?"

He held her gaze, his expression warm and happy. "Probably not."

"So I can't believe what you say? That's no help."

"You can always believe what I say. If I don't mention that the food's good, then I'm not crazy about it, but that doesn't mean it's bad. Everybody has stuff they don't like."

Folding her arms on the table, she pinned him with a look. "Name one thing. I haven't found a single dish yet that you actually said you didn't care for."

"I'm not wild about anything with prunes in it."

"Really? Why is that?"

"After my mom died, my dad took over the kitchen and started reading up on vitamins in food and what people should and shouldn't eat. I think he figured that it was up to him to keep me alive by making sure I ate right."

Her heart ached for the seven-year-old boy and his earnest father, who had probably been a young man himself, maybe even younger than Matthew was now. "I assume he was a big fan of prunes."

"Oh, yeah. We ate them out of the box, and we ate them stewed. We ate them cut up on cereal, and I think once he mixed them into the meatloaf. That was the only time I wouldn't eat what he put in front of me, and he finally admitted maybe prunes didn't go so well in meatloaf." He chuckled and shook his head. "I vowed when I moved out that given a choice in the matter, I'd never eat another prune."

"Don't blame you."

He ate quietly for a few minutes before glancing up at her. "I've never told anyone about my dad and the prunes. It feels good to talk about him. Thanks for listening."

"My pleasure." She longed to go over and wrap her arms around him, but that might be interpreted as feeling sorry for him. She didn't, but it was a tender and private little story and she felt closer to him because he'd told it.

"I feel more relaxed here than I have in a long time."

"I'm glad."

"Part of it's the ranch house, and specifically this kitchen, but most of it is you."

At the honest respect in his eyes, warmth spread through her, and this time it had less to do with sex and more to do with a deepening friendship. "That's a very nice thing to say."

"It's true. You have a nurturing, calming presence that I've cherished from the first day we met."

"And here I thought you were hot for my body."

"I was. I am. But I also like just being with you, sitting across the table talking about things."

"I love hearing that." She sighed. "I feel the same, which means it's going to be hell when we have to say goodbye in six days."

"Six days? Is that all?"

She gestured to the wall calendar. "You can count them for yourself. Mary Lou and Watkins come back on Saturday afternoon, and my plane leaves Sunday. I'm due back at work Monday morning."

"I don't know why I thought we had more time."

She smiled. "Wishful thinking?"

"That would be it." He planted both hands on the table and pushed himself upright. "In that case, we need a little less talk and a lot more action around here."

She drained her wineglass and stood, too. "Did you have something specific in mind?" She knew exactly what he had in mind, but she loved teasing him.

He carried the dishes to the sink. "Yeah, I thought we'd play cards."

"Really?"

"Yes, really." He loaded everything in the dishwasher. "I carry a deck in my duffel bag, and I've been practicing my card-shark skills in the bunkhouse every night, so I think I'm ready to challenge you to a game."

"Of what?"

"Poker, of course. That's what all manly cowboys play."

She knew he was up to something, but she hadn't quite figured out what. "In case you hadn't noticed, I'm not a cowboy, and I'm definitely not manly."

"I'm aware of those things, but you can still play poker."

"What if I don't know how?"

He glanced over his shoulder and grinned. "Even better."

"I don't see why that would be better. You'll spend all your time teaching me how to play. That won't be any fun for you."

"Oh, yes, it will." He dried his hands on a towel and came toward her. "Ready to play some cards?"

"I don't think it'll be fun for me, either. If you're really good at it, and I'm really terrible, then you'll win all the time."

Looping an arm around her shoulders, he guided her toward the bedroom. "With the game I have in mind, we can both end up winners."

"How?"

"You'll see." Turning, he closed the bedroom door, which created the sense of privacy they'd both come to cherish. Then he walked over to his duffel bag and crouched down to sort through its contents.

She took advantage of the action to admire the way his faded jeans hugged his buns. With a view like that to inspire her, she lost all interest in learning some silly card game. She couldn't imagine why he was suggesting it when they could find so many more interesting ways to amuse themselves.

He rose to his feet, card deck in hand. He tucked it into his shirt pocket and walked over to sit in the suede chair. "Take off your shoes." He pulled off one of his boots. "We'll play on the bed."

"I can think of plenty of ways to play on the bed that

don't involve cards." But she humored him and nudged off her shoes before climbing onto the quilt.

He sat cross-legged facing her and took the pack of cards out of his shirt pocket. "So you've never played any kind of poker?"

"Nope."

"Then this is a good place to start. The French call it *tisonnier deshabillé*."

"Which means?"

"Strip poker."

12

AFTER THIRTY MINUTES and much hilarity, Matthew had things pretty much the way he'd wanted them. Aurelia was down to her skimpy little panties and all he'd given up was his belt. Watching her entire body turn pink with frustration whenever she lost a hand was the most fun he'd ever had playing cards.

She was catching on to the game, though, so he decided to let her win a couple to bolster her confidence. After that he was minus his socks. Then she surprised the hell out of him by winning on her own without him having to lay off his game.

His shock must have shown, because she started gloating. "Didn't expect me to win that time, did you?" She preened and fluffed her hair, which fell to her shoulders now that she'd had to give him the clip she'd used to hold it on top of her head. "Take off your shirt. I'm dealing."

Every time she did that, he wished he'd thought of playing strip poker days ago. Aurelia dealing cards topless would give any man with a pulse an instant erection. The jiggle factor was outstanding.

She finished dealing and glanced at him. "Well? Why isn't your shirt gone?" She picked up her hand.

"Sorry. Got distracted." He popped the snaps on his shirt and took it off.

"Mmm, nice."

He thought she was talking about her cards until he looked over and discovered she was ogling his chest. He shook his head. "I don't get what's so special. Now *your* chest is a work of art, but mine is just…there."

"You're a man. Of course you don't get it. But a woman sees those pecs and abs and turns all juicy inside."

"I'm obviously happy about that, especially in your case, but I still don't get it."

"Never mind." She made a flapping motion with her hand. "Just play cards. I want those jeans off, too."

"Nope. Your panties are going down." Except his hand was crap. He'd have to bluff if he expected to win this one.

But a bluff only worked if the opponent believed it, and damned if Aurelia didn't see right through him. She'd come to know him so well that his poker face didn't work on her. She won the hand.

"Jeans," she said. "Make them disappear."

He had to leave the bed to shuck them, and sadly, it was his deal. The game was much more interesting when Aurelia did that job. He shuffled and dealt the cards. Apparently his luck had shifted about the time Aurelia became a whiz at the game, because he was in trouble again.

He really needed to win this one, and he didn't have the cards to do it. In his mind, once her panties were gone, the game was over. He wasn't going to make her play for his briefs. He'd gladly give them up.

But he wasn't convinced she'd have the same strategy. From the way she was reacting to this contest, if he lost again, she'd make him suffer until he got the hand that would strip her of those panties. He had a bad habit of underestimating Aurelia, and he should have learned by now not to risk it.

As he'd feared, she had the cards and played them like a pro. "I do believe I've stripped you naked, Tredway," she said. "So what now?"

"As the winner, you could graciously agree to take yours off, too."

She shuffled the cards and looked very smug. "So it's my choice?"

"Well, yeah, but I think—"

"Then we'll keep playing until you finally win a hand, thus earning the right to have me remove said panties."

He groaned. "So you're going to make me suffer?"

"You were the one who had the bright idea of playing strip poker, or...what did you call it?"

"Forget what I called it. I was trying to be cute and made it up. Listen, how about if we put the cards away and just—"

"Nope." Her green eyes sparkled with mischief. "I'm going to make you work for it, cowboy." She dealt the cards, and when she was finished, she lowered her gaze to his crotch. "You certainly seem motivated to win a hand."

"Don't mock."

"Oh, I'm not. Not at all. That's a beautiful piece of

equipment you have there. Now if you could only win a hand of poker, you could put it to good use."

Matthew blew out a breath. "You're depriving yourself, too, you know."

"I know." Her tone was saucy. "But since this was your idea, I'm enjoying the way it turned out. I'm on a power trip."

He grimaced. "I can tell." Desperation made him reckless, and he lost a hand he should have won. As he dealt the next one, he forced himself to concentrate. She was not an experienced player. He could do this.

The tide turned. He got cards and she got cocky. He managed to keep lust at bay long enough to play his hand with finesse.

He had her, and once he was sure of it, he casually reached for the condom packet lying on the bedside table.

"Don't count your chickens," she said.

"My chickens are rounded up and in the coop." As he threw down his winning hand face-up, he felt like beating his chest in a primitive display of victory. But instead, he glanced over at her and smiled. "Panties off, sweetheart." He ripped open the condom package. "It's show time."

AURELIA HADN'T EXPECTED to have fun playing cards, but strip poker was a blast. She'd pretended to be upset when she lost, but in reality, having a chance to tease Matthew with a little shimmy here and a little shake there had only added to her enjoyment of the game. Winning enough hands to strip him naked before he'd been able to do the same to her had been pure luck, although she'd never tell him that.

Then she'd made him work for his ultimate prize, and when she pulled her black panties off, she tossed them to him. "Your trophy, sir."

He caught them in one hand. "Quite damp, aren't they?"

"I might have become a little bit excited while we were playing."

"Seems so." He tossed the panties on the bedside table. "I might have to keep those for a souvenir."

"For your perseverance, I suppose."

"You really made me work for this." He dropped to his hands and knees and moved forward, as if stalking her.

"Fitting, considering you expected to win all along." She mimicked his stance. They circled each other, maintaining eye contact. She'd pushed him to the limit, and at some point he would spring and pin her to the mattress.

She was more than ready. Her nipples ached and her thighs were moist. Matthew brought out a side of her that she'd never known existed. But then, she'd never experienced the raw masculinity of a man who was more comfortable in boots, jeans and a cotton shirt than he would ever be in a suit and tie.

He'd spoiled her for ordinary men, and she knew that was the danger in becoming involved with somebody like Matthew. She'd taken the risk, and she'd do it again. This level of passion was well worth it.

His voice thrilled her with its restrained urgency. "You're taunting me, Aurelia."

"Am I?"

"Yes, but that's okay. I have good reflexes."

"So do I."

"But mine are better." With that he pounced.

She struggled because she knew he expected her to, and they rolled and wrestled on the bed, scattering covers and pillows, building the excitement. Twisting in his arms, she relished every contact with that hard body of his.

He was obviously using only a small portion of his strength, because if he'd really wanted to subdue her, he could have done it in seconds. Instead he let her think that she had a chance against him.

And then, suddenly, his arm tightened around her. Before she quite knew what he was doing, he'd brought her to her knees again as he moved behind her. Breathing hard, he leaned over and murmured in her ear, "Like this, tonight." It was not a request.

His commanding tone thrilled her. He took her in one sure movement, thrusting deep, removing any last trace of reserve she'd unknowingly clung to. They made love as if they were creatures in the wild, and she gave herself to him as she'd never given herself to a man before. Lifting her hips, she opened her thighs and invited him to claim her as his.

Almost before she realized it, she was coming, responding instinctively to his rapid strokes. He followed soon after, driving into her one last time, holding her hips steady to receive him. She felt him pulse within her body, felt his shudder and the deep moan of release.

He held her there for a few precious seconds, and then he wrapped his arms around her and rolled them both down to the crumpled sheets. They lay panting, spooned together, still connected.

His hands cupped her breasts and squeezed gently. His breath was warm against her shoulder. "Thank you."

"I loved it."

"Me, too."

Her breathing slowed, and though she fought to stay awake, she drifted inevitably toward sleep. In that twilight before she went completely under, she was vaguely aware that Matthew left the bed, which left her chilled. Then he was back. Gathering her close, he pulled the quilt over them, and she surrendered to oblivion.

She woke up to the sound of the shower in her small bathroom. Cowboys rose at dawn, she'd discovered, and anyone who slept with them had better get used to it. In her opinion, the advantages of spending the night with Matthew far outweighed this small disadvantage.

Sitting up in bed, she used her fingers to comb some of the tangles from her hair. As her eyes adjusted to the pale light, she glanced at Matthew's deck of cards on the nightstand and smiled. She might need to study up on poker so that she could get off to a better start next time.

And yet, what was the point, really? They only had a handful of nights left, and then she couldn't be sure when and if she'd see him again. Becoming a poker expert didn't make much sense when she had no desire to play the game, naked or clothed, with anyone but Matthew.

Picking up the cards, she shuffled them, smoothed the sheet and laid out a hand of solitaire. She liked handling the cards, because they belonged to Matthew. She had the silly urge to ask if she could keep them.

Cards, and specifically the game of poker, would forever remind her of him. So would all the recipes he'd helped her convert to cowboy-friendly dishes. In fact, that could be the hook for her blog—turning gourmet dishes into something the whole family would eat. Others were already doing something similar, but she'd give it her own personal twist and reference her experience feeding cowboys and teenagers on a Wyoming ranch.

Now that she'd become familiar with the Last Chance, she hoped Aunt Mary Lou would invite her back to visit. She wouldn't mind learning to ride, although while she was the full-time cook she hadn't felt she could spare the time for that. She was a rank beginner and would need lots of instruction before she'd feel comfortable on a horse.

Then the man who would make the perfect riding teacher walked into the room rubbing his wet hair with a towel. She knew he felt at home with her because he hadn't bothered to wrap a second one around his hips. She'd lost all modesty with him, too. She wondered if being apart and seeing each other only occasionally would change that. Probably.

"Couldn't resist getting your hands on those cards again, I see." He grinned at her. "Next thing I know you'll be dealing in Vegas."

"How did you guess?" She allowed herself to admire his finely sculpted body because, after all, she wouldn't have much longer to do that.

"The seven of hearts can go on the eight of spades." With regret she changed her focus from a naked

Matthew to the solitaire game. She played the seven of hearts as he'd suggested.

"And now the six of—"

"Hey." She made a shooing motion with her free hand. "Get your own solitaire game."

"Can't." He started drying his hair with the towel again. "You have my cards."

"You weren't using them."

"More's the pity." He looped the towel around his neck and walked over to his duffel bag. "But I gotta go to work. Thanks for washing some things for me yesterday, by the way. I was running low."

"Welcome." The interchange was so sweetly domestic that it made her throat ache.

"I had an idea in the shower."

"What's that?" She played three cards in a row and began to think she'd win the game.

"Blogs can be written from anywhere."

"Right." She uncovered exactly the card she needed and slapped it triumphantly onto the pile. "Which is why it's so perfect for you. You can travel and still do it."

"So could you."

"What do you mean?" Ah, there was the jack of spades. Perfect.

"You could combine blogging and travel. You could call it *A Fork in the Road*."

Lifting her head, she looked over at him. He'd just finished putting on his jeans and now he sat in the suede chair to pull on his boots. "Matthew, what are you talking about?"

He pulled on one boot and glanced up at her. "Your

blog. Wouldn't it be great to go all over the world trying different regional recipes and then blogging about it?"

"Maybe for somebody else." She frowned. "I'm surprised you'd say something like that when you know I'm not into traveling."

"But you're into cooking, and you love trying different foods and recipes. Just think, you could talk to the owners of little cafés in out-of-the-way villages and find recipes nobody else knows about. Eventually you could do a book based on—"

"Matthew, did you hit your head on the shower nozzle? You're the traveler, not me." Her people weren't good travelers. A train trip across the country years ago had left her grandparents broke when someone stole their money. Her parents had flown to Chicago once and had barely made it out of a burning hotel room. An aunt and uncle got hopelessly lost attempting to find the St. Louis Arch and then their car's transmission had blown out.

She'd never, ever, aspired to a life of travel, which sounded miserable and scary. But she wasn't sure he'd understand, so she brought up a different objection. "I have a job in a bank, and that's how I support myself. Even if I wanted to try this crazy idea of yours, which I don't, I couldn't afford to quit my job and jaunt around collecting recipes and writing blogs."

He pulled on his other boot. "What if you didn't have to worry about the money angle? Would that make a difference? Because I sure see this as being a lot of fun for you, and it would make the blog a surefire hit."

Suddenly her tummy didn't feel very good. "Are you

saying that if I write the blog from Nebraska I'm wasting my time?"

"No, I'm not saying that at all. But I was in the shower, and the blog title *A Fork in the Road* came to me, and it's...a really good idea."

"I'm sure it is." And here she'd thought they were so much in sync. "But not for me." And because she didn't feel up to jumping on board with his plan, she felt somewhat diminished.

"I just figured I should throw it out there."

"I can see that you did, but it's totally impractical. You blithely eliminated the money problem, but that's only one of the big obstacles. I have some savings, but I'm not willing to quit my job and blow them on something that might never generate an income."

His gaze was steady. "I eliminated the money problem because if you liked the idea, I was going to take care of the expenses."

She stared at him as she worked to process that statement. "I have a feeling there's something else going on here."

Blowing out a breath, he stood and walked to the closet where she'd hung his shirts. "Of course there is, but first I needed to find out if you were at all interested. You're not, so that's the end of it."

Her heart raced. He was clearly disappointed by her response. The whole line of his body had gone from relaxed to tense. "Matthew, why did you ask me if I wanted to do a traveling cooking blog when you know I don't like to travel?"

Pulling a shirt off the hanger, he put it on without facing her. "It was a mistake."

"But why?"

"I woke up this morning with a feeling of dread, knowing we only have a few days left." He snapped his shirt with short, jerky movements. "Apparently I'm... I'm not okay with that. I know what we agreed, and obviously I need to man up and accept reality."

"You wanted me to travel with you?" Now that was a heartbreaker of a concept. "But you said you wouldn't ask a woman to trail around after you and try to fit her life into yours."

"Yeah, I know." Tucking his shirt into his jeans, he grabbed his belt from a hook inside the closet and threaded it through the belt loops. As he buckled it, he turned back to her. "But I thought if you were involved in the cooking and experimentation with recipes, you'd be happy with your job and I'd be happy with mine, and it would all...work."

Her eyes misted as she shook her head. "You've got the wrong girl."

His troubled gaze found hers, and gradually his expression softened. "Aurelia, would you at least think about it? I know it's a big step, but you were ready to reject the blog idea until you gave it some thought."

"That's quite a bit different."

"I suppose, but...just let yourself think about it." Without waiting for her answer, he left the room.

Taking a long, shaky breath, she gazed unseeingly at the solitaire game spread out in front of her. She didn't have to think about it.

Because he'd been traveling the world for years, he had no idea the monumental life change he'd asked her to consider. She couldn't do it. He might be dreading their eventual parting, but it was for the best. She wasn't the one for him.

13

MATTHEW SOMETIMES ATE a quick breakfast that Aurelia fixed for him, but this morning he'd wanted to let her sleep. On days he didn't eat with her, he usually grabbed something from the bunkhouse kitchen. Today he didn't feel like eating, period, and for a man who cherished his food, that was significant.

He'd seriously miscalculated when he'd chosen to become involved with Aurelia. She might be the only woman in the world who could make him regret his choices as he yearned to have it all—career, life partner, even family. Desperate not to lose her, he'd come up with a plan, and she'd flat-out rejected it.

Although he wasn't giving up without a fight, his chances didn't look good. Her uncompromising expression as he'd left the bedroom had told him that much. She'd given him nothing to work with, no hint that she might consider his suggestion.

If she refused even to consider it, he wasn't sure how well he'd be able to adjust. He'd always prided himself on being able to roll with the punches, but she had the power to deliver a knockout blow. And he'd given her that power by falling for her. While in the shower, he'd come to the startling conclusion that he was head over heels in love with this woman. There was no changing that now.

He sought refuge in the one place that had always comforted him—a horse barn. Because he'd skipped breakfast, he made it to the barn ahead of the cowhands. Butch and Sundance greeted him enthusiastically, probably because they thought he'd feed them.

"Sorry, guys. If I feed you that'll just cause confusion." He stopped to pet them, though. Butch, a tan short-haired dog of indeterminate ancestry, and Sundance, a black dog with curly hair and no visible pedigree, had been strays until the Chance family took them in.

Matthew admired the big-hearted spirit of this ranch and hoped to come back. But if he did, the place wouldn't be the same without Aurelia. He sighed and started down the aisle between the stalls. Houdini's was at the far end.

The horses all pricked up their ears and looked expectant as he came by. "Can't feed you, either," he told them. "Some of you may be on special diets. I'm not going to take a chance on messing that up."

A couple of them nickered in protest, but the rest went back to foraging for whatever they'd missed from last night's meal.

Houdini stuck his head over the stall door, clearly welcoming Matthew. That kind of affection was a very good sign. Matthew couldn't give himself all the credit. In the days following Lester's successful ride, Matthew had gradually allowed the other boys to take a turn. The socializing had been very good for the horse.

Houdini also stayed in his stall these days, not so much out of choice as his inability to break out. Matthew didn't kid himself that Houdini had abandoned his escape-artist leanings. Working with Emmett Sterling, Matthew had devised a latch that the horse couldn't open, at least not yet.

Standing by the stall door, he scratched along the base of Houdini's mane and stroked his velvet muzzle. "Females," he muttered. "Can't live with 'em, can't live without 'em."

Houdini snorted.

"I should probably be grateful, though. I still get to have sex the old-fashioned way, but once you're in the stud program, you'll be mounting a dummy instead of a mare. I can't believe that's much fun."

Houdini gazed at him with his liquid brown eyes.

"Yeah, you don't know what I'm talking about yet, but you will soon enough. Today might be the day, in fact. I was hired primarily so that you'd become the proud papa of a bunch of registered Paints, so you and I need to see if you'll be cooperative and mount that dummy."

Houdini pawed the floor of his stall.

"Don't get too excited, yet. I'll have to discuss it with Emmett."

"Did I hear my name mentioned?" The foreman walked through the open doorway of the barn.

"Just the man I need to talk to," Matthew said.

Emmett touched his hat in greeting. "You're up

early." He came toward Matthew with a slightly bow-legged stride.

"Lots to do today."

"Always." Tall and lean, Emmett was the quintessential seasoned cowboy, his face lined from years of working with horses out in the elements. His neatly trimmed mustache, which was starting to gray along with his dark hair, made him look even more authentic. "What did you need to discuss with me?"

"Houdini's made good progress with his training in the corral, but considering that he's destined to be a stud, we should probably find out if he's mellowed enough that we can get him to mount a dummy."

"As a matter of fact, Clay asked me about that yesterday, and I promised him a progress report."

"I've never seen the collection process, although I have a fair idea of what goes on. Do you think Houdini's ready?"

"One way to find out. I can see if Clay's available this morning."

"That would be great." Matthew had first met Clay Whitaker, who ran the stud program for the Last Chance, during his first morning on the ranch. Since then Clay had been busy dealing with semen shipments and they'd had no chance for a conversation. Clay was also Emmett's son-in-law following a spring wedding to Emmett's daughter Emily.

"Even if Clay's busy, he'll probably make time," Emmett said. "He's eager to get Houdini into the program. The horse has excellent bloodlines."

"But this will be one portion of Houdini's training that the kids don't need to be part of. If they find out about it, they might want to, though. Houdini's become almost like a pet to them."

"Let's just avoid the problem," Emmett said. "I'll get a couple of the hands to take those boys on a fence-mending detail this morning. Then you can let them ride Houdini this afternoon."

"That'll work. I'm going to take a turn on him, myself. Now that he's familiar with a bridle and a Western saddle, having me topside shouldn't faze him. It's about time to put the finishing touches on this project."

Emmett gave him a speculative glance. "I didn't think you were in that much of a hurry."

"You mean because of Aurelia?" No point in pretending not to know what Emmett was talking about.

"Yep. I thought you'd want to stay on here until she left for Nebraska."

"I'm not sure that's a good idea anymore."

"You two have a spat?"

"Not exactly. We just…I dunno." Matthew tilted his hat back with his thumb and looked at Emmett. "Our sticking point seems to be travel. I'm going to guess you're not much of a traveler yourself."

"That'd be a good guess."

"And why is that?"

"No point in it. Everything I want is right here." He stroked a finger over his mustache. "That's where you and I are different. You have a hankering for faraway places. I like my regular routine and my familiar surroundings."

"And I get that. For you, it makes perfect sense, because working on a ranch is your dream. But I can't figure that working in a bank is Aurelia's dream. She's never once talked about her job."

The foreman paused as if weighing Matthew's comment. "She strikes me as a girl who likes security," he said finally. "Her job could make her feel secure."

"Hell, I could give her all the security she wants. If she'd travel with me, she could search out recipes from around the world, and then collect them into an international cookbook. Or two cookbooks. A whole damned series of cookbooks! You've seen how creative she is. Doesn't that seem like something she'd be happy doing?"

"She might, but if she's spent her whole life in the same place, going on some grand adventure with you could feel like jumping off a cliff."

"But I'd be there to catch her."

Emmett's gaze was sympathetic. "You know that, but she may not believe it, at least not yet. It takes time, son, just like with horses. People can't change their ways overnight any more than a horse can."

"But I thought by now she'd trust me more." He gestured toward Houdini. "He does."

"Of course he does. You haven't asked him to leave everything he's used to."

Matthew sighed. "Damn it all, you're right. I pushed her and she pushed back. I guess I should have expected that instead of thinking she'd grab hold of the idea and run with it."

"Maybe if you back off she'll come around."

"Maybe."

"Or not. You don't want to force a relationship with

a woman if it's wrong. I did that with my ex, and Jack's dad, Jonathan, did the same with Diana."

"Yeah, I picked up on that story. Where is Jack's half brother, by the way? Am I going to get to meet him?"

"Probably not. Summer's busy for wilderness guides, and he wants to earn as much as he can now that he's going to be a married man."

Matthew nodded. "Marriage. It's quite a step, isn't it?"

"Oh, yeah."

"Thanks for the advice. You obviously understand women better than I do."

"I wouldn't say that." Emmett's smile was rueful. "And Pam Mulholland *definitely* wouldn't say that. She's nearly lost patience with me."

Matthew remembered listening to the cowhands talk about that ongoing drama. Pam owned the bed-and-breakfast down the road, and she'd had her eye on Emmett for years. Because she had more money in the bank than Emmett, he resisted any suggestion of marriage. He was willing to carry on an affair, but apparently tying the knot would make him feel like a kept man.

Matthew's issues with Aurelia made him prone to side with Pam, the person with the money. He'd bet Pam was as eager to share her wealth with Emmett as Matthew was to share his with Aurelia. "The hands all say she's crazy about you."

"Don't know why." Emmett's voice was gruff. "I'm just an old saddle tramp. She could do a whole lot better."

From Matthew's standpoint, any woman would be lucky to hook up with a guy like Emmett. He was kind, generous and principled. "For what it's worth, I think you're selling yourself short." He smiled. "But hey, considering how messed up my love life is right now, I have no business meddling in anyone else's."

Emmett chuckled. "Are you saying we're the blind leading the blind?"

"Could be. Maybe we should concentrate on matters we do know something about, like horses. Much simpler."

"Ain't that the truth."

But as the morning progressed, Matthew had trouble following his own orders. No matter how hard he tried to shove thoughts of Aurelia to the back of his mind, they kept intruding. Maybe it was partly because he was in the semen-collection shed, and a guy faced with that procedure couldn't help thinking of sex. After the past week and a half, Matthew couldn't think of sex without thinking of Aurelia.

Clay Whitaker, a conscientious guy who knew horses and the science of semen collection, gave his complete attention to convincing Houdini he should mount the cloth dummy.

"I can see why he's not going for it," Matthew said. "It's like the equine version of a blow-up doll."

"While a hot babe waits in the next room behind a locked door," Clay added.

Matthew laughed. "Exactly." A teaser mare in season was tethered in a wooden pen at the back of the shed where Houdini could smell her but couldn't get to her.

"At least he's excited by the mare, which is helpful," Clay said. "Houdini wants her with the heat of a thousand suns."

"But he's not buying the cloth-dummy aspect," Matthew said. "Frankly, in his place, neither would I."

Clay laughed. "There are many times while I'm doing this job that I want to turn the stallion loose and let him have some real fun."

"Don't blame you."

"But if I did, I'd get fired, and rightly so. That mare is not the one who's supposed to get Houdini's semen. We have customers who are willing to pay a good amount of money so that Houdini impregnates their mare and not ours."

Matthew wiped his forehead on his sleeve. "How long should we keep this up?"

"Truthfully? I think at this point we might be wasting our time. Besides, it's nearly noon and Aurelia will be serving lunch. Let's try him again tomorrow morning. He might have a change of heart between now and then."

"Works for me." Timing and patience seemed to be the order of the day. "Sorry we couldn't get him up there."

"No worries. He's a thousand percent easier to handle than he was two weeks ago. I would have been amazed if we'd succeeded the first time. But once we convince him, then it'll get a lot easier. Some satisfaction is better than none."

"I'll take your word for it." Matthew had always been an all-or-nothing kind of guy.

"I'll lead the mare out the side door if you'll lead Houdini out the front."

"Sure thing." But Houdini planted his feet when Matthew tried to coax him out of the shed. He didn't want to give up when he thought he might still get a shot at the mare. Matthew decided to wait until Clay and the mare were out of the shed.

As the pretty little brown and white Paint mare left, Houdini trumpeted his disappointment.

"I feel your pain, my friend," Matthew said. "It sucks to have the doors of paradise slammed in your face."

FOR THE FIRST TIME since Matthew had arrived at the Last Chance, Aurelia dreaded seeing him come into the dining room for lunch. Sure, her heart beat faster as it always did, but bubbles of happiness no longer fizzed in her veins. When his gaze met hers, his expression was guarded.

She hated that, but didn't know how to fix it short of leaping on the bandwagon he'd rolled out for her this morning. Because she wasn't planning to do that, their relationship was bound to be strained. She served the meal, a rice-and-chicken dish with roots in a Creole recipe she'd found and he'd helped her modify.

Usually she could hardly wait to get his reaction when he finally tasted the results of his consultation and her cooking skills. But today, any comments on her food would remind them both of their discussion this morning. She wished she could erase it from her memory and return to the easy camaraderie they'd enjoyed before he'd come up with his suggestion to completely alter her life.

Still, she couldn't bear not to speak to him. She'd figured out from snatches of conversation that the boys had been sent out to repair the fence line while Matthew did some additional work with Houdini that didn't include the kids.

As she was clearing the plates, she paused beside his chair. "Did your morning go well with Houdini?"

"Not as well as Clay and I had hoped."

Then she understood. Clay was in charge of the semen operation for the ranch, so if he'd been working with Matthew, the two of them must have tried unsuccessfully to collect some from Houdini. "I'm sorry to hear that."

As she imagined two big strapping cowboys trying to milk semen from a stallion, she had to press her lips together to keep from laughing. No doubt they weren't amused by their lack of success. She was liable to insult them if she wasn't careful.

"We'll try again tomorrow morning."

"Good." She hurried away before he could tell she was struggling to control herself.

Later, after the dining room emptied, she came out of the kitchen with a damp cloth to wipe down the tables. Matthew stood there, the only person left. Apparently he wasn't going to walk into the bedroom and check his email as he usually did, and neither would he quietly leave the house and avoid the conversation completely.

She shouldn't be surprised that he'd choose to deal with her in a straightforward way. He was that kind of man, someone who faced things head-on. He said what he thought and asked questions when he needed an answer. She admired that.

His first comment had nothing to do with email. He went straight to the heart of the matter. "I thought I'd better check and find out if you still want me to come up after dinner."

Her breath caught as she realized how easily their connection would slip away if she told him not to bother. But even though they were more awkward with each other now, she wasn't ready to let him go. Not yet.

"Of course I want you to come up," she said. "We have tomorrow's menus to plan, for one thing."

His gaze searched hers. "I'm happy to help with that, but if you'd rather I didn't stay, then I can move my stuff out of your—"

"I want you to stay," she said quietly. "I realize we don't see things exactly the same, but that doesn't mean I want you to move down to the bunkhouse. I like to think we still get along reasonably well."

"I like to think we do, too." Some of the tension eased from his shoulders. "So if you're sure…"

"Absolutely sure. Don't you need to check your email before you go back down to the corral?"

He shrugged as if that was the least of his worries. "It can wait."

That was a switch. He'd always been conscientious about email, because it was the main avenue for communicating with his clients. "Look, Matthew, don't alter your routine just because we had a little—"

"It really can wait, Aurelia." His blue gaze held hers. "I don't have to be constantly accessible to my clients. I realize now I might have given you that impression and it's not true."

"But it could be something critical."

"Then they'll call my cell phone and I'll get the message when I turn it on after my training session. I want you to know that I do take breaks. I take vacations."

"Good. I'm glad to hear it." How she missed the easy way they used to talk. Their conversation was so stilted now. "I hope you'll use one of them to come and visit me in Nebraska."

His smile was tinged with sadness. "That wasn't why I mentioned it."

"Then why did you?"

"I didn't want you to think I'm constantly on the move. There's this great cottage in Provence. I try to rent it at least a couple of times a year for a week or so. You'd love the kitchen. It's—"

"Matthew, don't."

He looked as if she'd slapped him.

The impression was so real that she reached up and touched his cheek. "I'm sorry. I know you love your life and you want me to love it, too. But you're wasting your breath."

He caught her hand. After holding it there for a moment, he let her go and stepped back. "No, I'm the one who should be sorry. You made your position clear and I need to honor that."

"You do understand, right?"

He nodded. "Yeah."

His answer lacked conviction, but she doubted he would ever truly understand, anyway.

He cleared his throat. "I'm planning to ride Houdini this afternoon. I don't know if you have time to come and watch, but this is the moment I've been working toward."

"Then I want to be there."

14

HE'D BLOWN IT WITH AURELIA...again. Standing inside the corral, Matthew rotated the boys on and off Houdini. Both the kids and the horse were so used to the riding exercise that Matthew only had to offer a suggestion here and there.

That left him more than enough time to consider his ill-advised comments to Aurelia. He'd promised himself he would leave the subject alone, and first chance he got, he was in there pitching, trying to convince her that life traveling with him would be a bed of roses.

In his mind, it would be. That little cottage in Provence was made for someone like Aurelia. Climbing roses around the front door, a kitchen garden, a small fireplace for chilly nights, paths to wander and vistas to explore—he ached to show it to her.

The place was on the internet. If he hadn't been so heavy-handed this morning and again at noon, he could have just *happened* to show her pictures of it while he was checking email. He could have led up to this whole plan more gradually, and maybe she would have reacted differently.

He had patience galore with animals, so logically he should have been able to apply the same principles to Aurelia. Except with animals, he'd never had a time limit. He'd always insisted that his clients give him as much time as he needed to create a transformation.

With Aurelia, the clock had started ticking from the moment they'd met, and now time was running out. He'd tried to ignore that fact, but she'd brought it up the night before and reminded him exactly how many days they had left. He'd panicked, and the resulting adrenaline rush had ramped up his natural problem-solving approach to life.

He loved his solution to their dilemma. He desperately wanted her to love it, too, because he believed it would work. She was a lot better suited to travel than she thought she was. She'd arrived at the ranch not knowing a soul other than her aunt.

By rights, Aurelia should have been lonely and homesick. Instead, by the time Matthew arrived, she'd settled in and made friends. Even more astonishing, she'd taken the risk of serving unusual food to people she didn't know.

Aurelia might think she needed the security of living in the same place and working in a safe job, but Matthew was convinced she'd flourish if she moved permanently out of her rut. Her experience at the Last Chance proved it to him.

He would have been able to make that argument, too, if he hadn't rushed his proposition. Now he didn't dare say a damned thing, because she'd stonewall him if he did. He'd handled this matter about as poorly as anyone possibly could.

"So when's the Big Dog gonna get on that nag?"

Recognizing the voice of one of the Chance brothers, Matthew glanced over toward the fence.

Jack, the oldest and most irreverent of the three, leaned against the top rail, his hat tilted back and a grin on his face. "I suppose we could always start offering pony rides for kids and scrap the idea of making him into a cutting horse."

Matthew smiled and walked over to the fence. "Just tell me which way you want to go, Jack. I'm here to help."

"Ah, you're doing a great job." Jack stuck out his hand. "Thanks."

"You're welcome." Matthew gripped Jack's hand. "But I'm not finished. There will be more schooling once I'm on him. I weigh a lot more than those boys, and I'll expect more from him than they do."

"I heard you were going to ride him this afternoon, so I decided to wander over and see if your butt stayed in the saddle."

"You're welcome to try him out first, if you want. I really don't expect any problems."

"Oh, no." Jack held up both hands. "You've put in the work. You deserve that first ride."

"And the humiliation if he doesn't do as he's told?"

"That, too."

"Assuming I get him to behave himself, are you okay with me taking him outside the corral?"

"You're the trainer. Your call."

Matthew nodded. "Thanks. I'd like to see how he does outside the fence."

"I can tell you this, he loves to run." He turned as

Tucker Rankin came out of the barn and started toward the corral. "Just ask that man. He chased Houdini all over the county on Christmas Eve."

"So I heard."

"Hey, Matthew." Tucker lengthened his stride. "Heard you were going to ride him today."

"That was my thought." He glanced at Jack. "Word seems to have spread."

"We're always up for a show."

Matthew glanced at Jack and Tucker. "You both think he's going to embarrass me somehow, don't you?"

"I hope he doesn't," Tucker said. "I have ten bucks riding on you giving us a clean run."

"I see." Matthew turned to Jack. "And how did you bet?"

"This is one tricky horse. He seems to love kids, but I'm not so sure he's going to love hauling you around. I think he's going to challenge you."

Matthew laughed. "You must not think I'll meet that challenge."

"I'm sure you're a good rider. But I've observed this animal for months, and he likes to have the last word. Fortunately he has a weak spot for kids, but you're no kid."

"No." Matthew glanced over at the horse. "But we'll straighten that out real quick." If he was drawing a crowd, he'd probably better get this handled. He turned back to Jack, curious about one thing. "How are you going to keep score?"

"Well, if he tosses you in the dirt—"

"Not going to happen."

"Okay, then we'll need an impartial judge to decide

whether you came out ahead of the horse or vice versa." Jack looked over at the barn. "And here comes the perfect man for the job. Emmett Sterling."

"I'll gladly take Emmett as the judge." Matthew started to walk away from the rail.

"I want to put ten bucks on Matthew." Aurelia hurried toward them waving a bill in the air and breathing hard, as if she'd run the distance from the house to the corral. "You haven't closed the betting, have you?"

"Always room for one more." Jack took the money she handed him.

Matthew appreciated the gesture and gave her a quick smile to tell her so, but it was a safe bet. He was encouraged that Aurelia believed in his horsemanship.

Gary happened to be up on Houdini as Matthew approached. The boy was allowing the horse to choose his own path, which wasn't the program Matthew had outlined for the kids, but he'd been distracted by the gathering crowd and hadn't noticed that Gary was letting Houdini do as he pleased.

Naturally the horse managed to get away with things while the teenagers rode him, although Lester was pretty good at making him mind. As for the other boys, Matthew caught what he could and let the rest go. On balance, including the teens in the training sessions had been a good thing for them and for Houdini. Matthew was prepared, though, for the stallion to try to control things once an adult rider was on board.

Gary dismounted with far more grace than when he'd first started riding Houdini several days ago. "I think he's warmed up pretty good, Mr. Tredway. Are you going to take him, now?"

"I think it's time to give that a try, don't you?"

Gary nodded enthusiastically. "Oh, you bet, Mr. Tredway. Listen, you probably don't need any tips from a kid like me, but every now and then, he might try to scrape you against the corral. You might want to watch out for that."

"Thanks, Gary." Matthew squeezed the boy's shoulder. "It's a big help when horsemen share that kind of thing."

Gary beamed. "Just thought you'd want to know. But he's a good horse. I think in his heart he means well."

"I'm sure he does." Matthew was used to having the kids interpret Houdini's moods and behaviors. Usually they assigned the horse their own qualities, like now. Sure, Houdini misbehaved now and then, but in his heart, he meant well, just like Gary.

Matthew found that incredibly touching, and he was more determined than ever to write a book geared to kids. Pete Beckett had created something special by bringing troubled teens to a ranch where they could interact with horses. Matthew wouldn't mind coming back in a different capacity next summer—as a facilitator between horses and kids.

But if he wanted to be invited back, he needed to nail this riding demonstration. His credibility was on the line, not to mention Aurelia's ten bucks. He didn't want to be responsible for losing any of her hard-earned cash, especially when he knew she was so security-minded.

He asked Gary to hold Houdini's bridle while he adjusted the stirrups. Houdini stood there like the most docile horse in the barn, but Matthew knew better. If Houdini had been trying to scrape Gary against the fence, he'd do that and more when he was asked to carry Matthew.

"Okay, Gary." Matthew put his booted foot in the stirrup. "Turn him loose."

Houdini snorted as he felt the extra weight settle onto his back. Matthew nudged him with both heels and clucked with his tongue. Houdini didn't move.

"So we're going to play this game." Matthew kicked him harder and flicked his rump with the end of the reins.

Houdini started off at a hard trot, the kind that would jar the fillings from a rider's back molars.

Matthew pulled him to a halt. "You can do better than that."

Houdini's ears flicked back and forth, so he was listening, and he certainly knew who was talking to him.

"I mean it, Houdini." He rubbed the horse's neck. "Smooth it out." He urged him forward again.

This time the trot was decent, but as Gary had predicted, Houdini made for the fence. With a firm hand on the reins, Matthew headed him away from the rail. In protest, Houdini began playing with the bit as if determined to be annoying.

Matthew nudged the horse back into a trot, and after a few minutes, into a canter. Once again Houdini made for the fence, but Matthew's grip on the reins and the steady pressure of his legs brought the horse back in line. Matthew kept him at a canter while they circled the corral a couple of times without Houdini trying to squeeze his legs against the fence.

Once Matthew was satisfied that the horse wouldn't try that maneuver again, he reined him in and asked if someone would open the gate. Houdini watched it open and fought the bit in an effort to go through.

Matthew kept him on a short rein. "When I say so, and not before." He held the prancing horse by the open gate for several seconds before letting him trot through.

Predictably, Houdini headed for the barn door, no doubt hoping for food. Matthew turned him down a pathway that led to an open meadow.

"You're taking a big risk!" Jack called after him. "He's going to try and run away with you!"

Matthew raised a hand in acknowledgment and held Houdini down to a trot as they entered the meadow. The horse's muscles bunched as if preparing for a charge, but Matthew kept control. "When I say so," he murmured to the horse. "And not before."

After several yards, he eased the horse into a canter, and still Houdini strained at the bit. After a few more lengths, Matthew let him run, but even then, he kept a commanding grip on the reins. Horse and rider raced over the meadow as grasses and wildflowers waved in the wind they created in passing.

At last Matthew slackened the reins in a gesture of trust. Houdini responded with a joyous burst of speed as if to say *yes, I like this. Yes!* Matthew lived for this moment of communion with the horses he trained. But once he'd achieved it, his work was done. Turning back toward the ranch, he kept Houdini at a canter for several lengths. Then he slowed the horse to a trot.

By the time they came in sight of the corral and the small crowd that had gathered there, Houdini was down to a walk, but it was more of a prance. He held his head and tail high as if he'd just won the Kentucky

Derby. Matthew smiled and patted his neck. "Enjoyed that, did you?"

Houdini snorted, obviously very pleased with himself.

As Matthew rode the horse over to the corral and dismounted, he accepted the congratulations of the cowhands and the Chance brothers.

Jack clapped him on the back. "And that's why they pay you the big bucks. This is one case in which I'm more than happy to lose a bet."

"Thanks, Jack."

Emmett gave him a thumbs-up. "Knew you could do it, son." He reached for Houdini's bridle. "Let me take this fellow and rub him down. Lester can help me."

Even though Matthew was used to taking care of the horse he'd ridden, he knew when to step back. "Thanks. I appreciate it."

Emmett grinned at him. "Now go deal with your public." He and Lester took Houdini into the barn.

"He sure can run, can't he?" Tucker came up to shake Matthew's hand. "At first I thought we'd have to send out a search party, but then you brought him back, no problem."

"He's a good horse," Matthew said. "I doubt you'll have any problem with him from now on." He looked around for Aurelia, and finally found her at the edge of the crowd.

Her smile trembled as she made her way over to him. "That was magnificent," she said. "You're doing exactly what you should be doing, Matthew. I'm so happy for you."

He would have loved to have her continue that wonderful praise with some dramatic statement that now she'd follow him anywhere, but after giving his arm a squeeze, she turned and walked back up to the house.

Lester approached, hugging a book to his chest and puffing. "I ran back to my room for this," he said. "Sarah helped me send away for it last week, and it just came today. Will you sign it?"

"Of course." Matthew glanced once more at Aurelia in hopes she might turn back because that ride had convinced her they should travel the world together. But she kept walking. Apparently she wasn't *that* impressed.

Lester moved closer, still clutching his book. "I also wanted to tell you something. Something good." He pitched his voice low, as if he didn't want anyone else to hear.

Crouching down, Matthew gazed into eyes alight with happiness. "What's up?"

"Mr. Beckett said I can stay." The boy quivered with excitement. "I have to keep quiet about it so the others don't get jealous, but Nick and Dominique are going to be my new foster parents."

Despite Matthew's personal misery, he was overjoyed for Lester. "That's wonderful. Absolutely wonderful."

"You can't say anything, though. It's a secret."

"I won't say a word." Matthew appreciated the trust Lester was placing in him. "Now I'd better sign that book before someone wonders what we're in a huddle about."

"Right." Lester thrust it toward him.

Matthew balanced a copy of *Think Like a Horse* on his knee and accepted the pen Lester had remembered to bring along. *To Lester,* he wrote on the title page, *A born horse trainer. It's been a pleasure working with you.* He signed his name and closed the book.

Gary sidled over looking forlorn. "Aw, I want a book."

That sentiment was echoed by all the other boys as they drew closer, but Lester had been the only one with the foresight to order a book last week so he'd have a chance of getting it before Matthew left the ranch.

"Lester thought ahead, guys," Matthew said. "I'm afraid you won't have time to order one, now. But I noticed the ranch had promotional postcards made up, so I'll sign one of those for each of you, including Lester, who can use his as a bookmark."

The kids seemed reasonably happy with that compromise, although all of them kept eyeing Lester's book, which he held on to as if he never intended to let it out of his sight.

Clay walked over and held out his hand. "Nice job."

"Thanks." Matthew accept Clay's warm handshake.

"Now all we need to do is accomplish the other task, and you can claim a hundred percent success."

"Right." Matthew wasn't about to tell him that all factors considered, he was a long way from feeling like a success. But he'd concentrate on Lester's good fortune and take solace from that.

15

As usual, Aurelia had her cookbooks spread out on the table in anticipation of Matthew's arrival. But for the first time, she felt as if she might be wasting his time with this project. Until this afternoon, she hadn't fully appreciated his talent.

Oh, sure, she'd read his book. She'd returned Sarah's copy because her new one had come in the same box with Lester's. Reading the book should have made her realize that she was sleeping with an international celebrity who had achieved fame because he was incredible at his job.

But the tone of the book was so humble that she hadn't quite realized that. Watching him with Houdini, however, had brought it home to her in a very dramatic fashion. Matthew deserved his worldwide reputation because the man flat-out knew how to deal with horses.

More than that, he'd been born with wings. Galloping across the meadow on Houdini he'd become a free spirit, the man who traveled the globe and wrote bestselling books, the man who had no business hooking up with an earthbound creature like her.

He must have temporarily lost his mind when he asked her to travel with him. He had a dazzling career going, and he didn't need to drag along a budding cookbook author. If she hadn't provided such outstanding sex, one of two things she felt extremely confident about, he would never have dreamed up such a plan.

She needed to let him back away from that idea without feeling a smidgen of obligation to her. Once he'd put some distance between himself and the hot sex they'd shared, he'd be relieved that he hadn't talked her into going with him. It would have been a terrible mistake for both of them.

When his knock came at the back door, her heart quickened as it always did at the prospect of seeing him. Closing the cookbooks and stacking them on the table, she walked through the laundry room to the back screen door. It wasn't full dark yet, but the porch light had clicked on.

Matthew stood illuminated by the golden glow, his face shadowed by the brim of his Stetson. He seemed taller to her now, more imposing. This was the man who'd maintained control of a fifteen-hundred-pound stallion as they'd raced together across the grasslands in a glorious blend of power and beauty.

Before this afternoon's display of his expertise, she'd thought of him as a horse trainer, a cowboy not so different from the other hands working on the ranch. To be fair, he'd portrayed himself that way by hanging out at the bunkhouse, playing cards with the guys and generally staying out of the limelight.

Not today. Maybe someone else could have made that ride on Houdini this afternoon, but Aurelia doubted it. The horse had tested Matthew, but the outcome had never been in doubt.

Matthew gave her a half smile. "Are you going to let me in?"

"Sure. Sorry." She opened the door and stepped back. "It wasn't locked."

"I know, but I always wait to be invited." Taking off his hat, he walked through the door.

For the first time she noticed that he had to duck slightly to make it inside. "That's because you have good manners. You—"

"Aurelia." With a groan he pulled her into his arms and crushed her mouth against his. His kiss was desperate, demanding.

She'd meant to be more reserved tonight and give him a chance to pull away, but she was helpless before his unexpected onslaught. She kissed him back with equal hunger. Even if he wasn't to be hers forever, she couldn't pretend that she didn't want him more than she'd ever wanted another man.

Tossing his hat onto a dryer, he gripped her bottom in his large hands and lifted her up against the bulge in his jeans. She wrapped her arms around his neck and her legs around his waist. Carrying her like that, his mouth still covering hers, he strode out of the laundry room, through the kitchen, and into the bedroom, where they fell to the bed.

Clothes flew, a condom was located, and then he was inside her. She rose to meet each deep thrust, her frenzy matching his. When he was making love to her with such urgency, the issues between them faded, leaving only this wonder, this connection, this…man.

She came in a rush of emotion and pleasure that she'd only known with him. He followed soon after, and she knew he'd waited for her, because that was the kind of lover, the kind of generous person, he was.

He gulped for air and gazed down at her in the soft lamplight. Then he frowned and began kissing her cheeks. "Don't cry," he murmured. "Please don't cry. It'll be okay. I'll make it be okay."

She hadn't realized she was crying, but now that he was kissing away her tears, she felt the dampness on her face. "It's not…because I'm sad."

"Then why?"

"I'm just so grateful for you, Matthew." Her voice was husky with tears. "So very grateful that we had this time together."

His frown deepened. "I wish you wouldn't talk as if we're never going to see each other again."

In fact, she had decided that would be for the best. She loved him, and that love ran so deep that a few days here and there over the course of a year would give her more pain than joy. She'd want more, and she couldn't have more.

"Aurelia, what's going on?"

"Nothing." She pulled his head down for a quick kiss. "Go take care of the condom, then we'll play some cards."

"We can't play strip poker. We've already stripped."

"Then maybe we can make up another game."

"Okay." He didn't sound as if he bought into her attempt to derail the conversation. "Be right back."

When he walked into the bathroom, she sat up, noticed that the room looked as if a bomb had gone off, and decided not to do anything about it. The cards were still sitting on the nightstand, so she picked them up and started shuffling.

"You weren't kidding." He climbed back into bed.

"Nope. We can play for…I know. Sexual positions. Whoever wins gets to choose." She placed the deck on the bed between them. "Cut the cards."

"No." He picked up the deck and set it behind him on the other nightstand. "I can't concentrate on a silly card game when what you said is still ringing in my ears. You're planning to end everything when the week's over, aren't you?"

She met his gaze. "I didn't say that." And she hadn't intended to tell him until the last day, but her guard had been down a moment ago. He was smart enough to pick up on the implication of her *I'm grateful for what we've had*. She still hoped to bluff her way out of it, though.

"Aurelia, I'm a native English speaker, and a writer, too. Being grateful for what we've *had,* past tense, tells me that you don't see any future tense coming into the picture. I thought we'd agreed to keep up with each other through our blogs so I could stop by and see you now and then."

She could evade the truth, but she couldn't tell him an outright lie. "I've decided that won't work for me."

His voice had taken on a definite edge. "Why not?"

The coward in her wanted to glance away while she delivered the next line, but she made herself look into his blue eyes. "Because after this banquet we've enjoyed together, grabbing a quick snack a few times a year would be very unsatisfying for me. I'd rather…" She couldn't figure out what she'd rather do if she couldn't have him, and that was part of the problem.

"You'd rather starve? Is that what you're saying?"

"I won't starve. You're being melodramatic."

"You're the one who started this food analogy. I'm just carrying it to its logical conclusion. And maybe you won't starve, but I'm not so sure about me."

She studied him, her heart full of love and admiration for all he was and all he would yet become. "You won't starve, Matthew. You're an incredible man who will flourish in any situation. I knew you were amazing, but after today's ride, I appreciate exactly how amazing."

He stared at her. "I was just doing my job. Nothing special."

"Oh, yes, it was special. *Is* special. I'm honored that I was part of your life for a little while."

"For God's sake. Would you stop talking like that? You're as talented in your field as I am in mine. And as for flourishing wherever you go, look at what you've done with this Last Chance gig."

"That was all you. You saved the day on that, too."

"Bull! When I arrived, you'd already won everyone's heart. They just weren't on board with the food. When you realized that, you adapted immediately. Also, unless I'm mistaken, you weren't racked by homesickness while you were here."

"No." She'd been a little surprised by that. "But I've called my folks a few times, and texted a few friends, so it's not like I've abandoned my life in Nebraska."

"Keeping in touch is normal and to be expected, especially if you've never left the state before. But face it,

Aurelia, you've bloomed where you were planted, even though you didn't know a single soul besides your aunt before you got here."

She shrugged. "It's a friendly place."

"The whole damned *world* is a friendly place! You would be a hit in Europe with your cooking skills, your sense of adventure, and your happy smile."

"I don't have a sense of adventure. Stop assigning me qualities you want me to have because it suits your purposes." And maybe this argument was just the one they needed to have, so he would distance himself from her.

"Sorry, but you had a sense of adventure long before I ever came on the scene. That's the only explanation for having the cojones to serve *brochettes aux rognons, de foie et lardons* to a bunch of cowhands. You are fearless, woman. Deny it all you want, but I know the truth."

"That's just food. It's not the same as flying all over creation."

"Well, it springs from the same basic desire for variety in your daily life, but I'll add another observation, since I'm on a roll analyzing your character."

She waved a hand at him. "Carry on. You don't have the foggiest idea what you're talking about, but don't let that stop you." And the more he raved, the more she'd dig in her heels, and that should finally send him packing. It was the best thing for both of them, even if she felt as if she were performing open-heart surgery on herself without anesthetic.

"I don't intend to stop talking, because I have to get this off my chest. You are without a doubt the most *stubborn* woman I've ever come across."

She folded her arms. "I prefer to say that I know myself a lot better than you know me."

"Why won't you even consider my idea? Hell, if you're half as good at banking as you are at preparing food, they'd be happy to rehire you if the traveling blog doesn't work out."

"Matthew, you are a traveling kind of person. It's who you are. I am a stay-at-home kind of person. It's—"

"Damn it, how do you *know?* You've never given the other kind of life a chance! Open up your eyes. It would be a perfect fit for you."

"No, it would be a perfect fit for *you,* or at least you imagine it would be, once you got me trained like you train a horse. But I'm not a horse, Matthew. You're wonderful at getting them to do what you want them to do, but those techniques won't work on me."

"I'm not trying to—oh, forget it." He climbed out of bed and began searching for his clothes. "You've made up your mind that it won't work, and the more I try to convince you that it will, the harder you'll argue. God, you're stubborn."

She sensed the crack opening up in her heart. It went right down the middle and soon she'd begin to feel the excruciating pain of losing him. Except she'd never really had him.

She'd wanted him to give up the notion they could travel together as a couple, and judging from the way he was stomping around and gathering his things, she'd succeeded. Someday he might be grateful to her for averting a disaster they'd both heartily regret. She'd never even been on a plane, let alone jetted around the world.

Right now, though, he was thoroughly pissed at her. He obviously wasn't used to a lack of cooperation. Maybe anger was a better emotion to take away with him than sadness, anyway.

"I'll stay in the bunkhouse tonight." His tone was carefully controlled. "It's possible I might be able to fly out tomorrow. I just have one more thing to accomplish with Houdini."

"Semen collection?"

"Yep." Duffel bag in hand, he paused at the bedroom door. "Listen, if you ever change your mind…"

"I won't."

"I know you won't, but if a miracle happens and you rethink this, Sarah has my cell phone number."

She didn't reply. She was too busy memorizing how he looked standing there in the doorway so she'd have that picture to carry locked in her broken heart.

"Goodbye, Aurelia."

She lifted a hand and gave him a little wave. Her throat had such a big lump in it she wouldn't have been able to speak even if she'd wanted to, which she didn't. Although she'd helped shove him out the door, she couldn't bear to say goodbye.

IT SEEMED AS IF EVERYTHING conspired to help Matthew get the hell out of Dodge. Houdini performed like an experienced stud the next morning, which Clay credited to yesterday's run through the meadow having worked off his bottled-up energy. Jack took Houdini on a short ride and pronounced him fit for training as a cutting horse.

Matthew's work was done, and he had no wish to hang around. When he'd returned to the bunkhouse the night before, the card game had still been in progress. The cowhands had plied Matthew with beer in an attempt to lighten the mood when they realized he'd ended things with Aurelia.

The attempt had been a dismal failure, and now the guys probably felt sorry for him. He was afraid to ask if he'd called out Aurelia's name in the middle of the night. It wouldn't have surprised him if he had.

Her rejection had carved a hunk out of him and he wasn't sure how soon he'd be back to normal. Maybe never. He might always long for her touch, her laughter and the lush feel of her body under his. He couldn't imagine himself with anyone else.

Late that morning, he avoided having to go in for lunch by asking Jeb to drive him to the airport. Jeb did his best to make conversation during the trip, but Matthew had trouble holding up his end, so it was a mostly silent ride. Matthew had let everyone think he'd booked a flight, but it wasn't true. His next job, at an estate outside London, didn't start for two weeks, so he had time on his hands and nowhere in particular to go.

After Jeb dropped him at the airport in Jackson, he located a rental counter and reserved an SUV for a week. Might as well drive the two hundred miles or so to Billings and check on his parents' gravesites. He hadn't done that in a while, and the drive would allow him some thinking time.

In the back of his mind lurked another motivation for staying in the general area. A small flame of hope still burned. Before she left Wyoming, Aurelia might come to her senses and give him a shot. If she did, and his cell phone rang, he didn't want to be far away.

He arrived at the cemetery in the middle of the afternoon. Parking the SUV, he walked between the rows of markers set flush with the grass until he found the two he was looking for. The grass was manicured and the headstones clear of debris, so apparently the management was living up to its promise of perpetual care.

Matthew had thought of bringing flowers, but knew they'd die quickly in the heat. He stood silently gazing down at the two engraved markers. His memory of his mother was dim and consisted mostly of the pictures he still had of her. But his father's image was clear.

The guy had done his level best to carry on after Matthew's mother died, but he'd struggled. Chainsmoking had been his crutch, and eventually it had killed him. Matthew had always wondered if his dad had secretly looked forward to the day he would end up here next to his wife.

Eloisa Ann Tredway, beloved wife of John Matthew Tredway, was etched into the granite on Matthew's left, and the reverse, John Matthew Tredway, beloved husband of Eloisa Ann Tredway, was on the right.

Beloved. Matthew had never quite grasped the numbing heartache his father must have felt when his wife died. And although leaving Aurelia was not even close to the same kind of tragedy, he understood his dad's grief a little better now.

No wonder his father hadn't been able to provide a sense of home and security. His wife's death had ended any dreams he'd had of those things. Matthew had learned early that he could survive without a warm family life and had eventually replaced any lingering feelings of emptiness with work and travel.

Until he'd met Aurelia, he'd never thought in terms of home and permanence for himself. Maybe a part of him had feared he'd end up blindsided like his father. He still couldn't picture himself settling down in one spot, but he desperately wanted to settle down with one woman.

He understood that happiness was never guaranteed, but that didn't mean he shouldn't reach for it, which meant reaching for Aurelia. Being with her felt like coming home after years of restless wandering. Whether she wanted to or not, she'd become his beloved.

His head snapped up as it suddenly occurred to him that he'd neglected to tell her that. It might not have made any difference, with her being so stubbornly set in her belief they couldn't have a life together. But he should have told her he loved her. And he hadn't.

16

THE DAY AUNT MARY LOU and her new husband Watkins were due back, Aurelia moved her things out of the bedroom and into a room upstairs. She'd sleep there tonight, and the next day someone would drive her to the airport, so she'd packed everything except a nightgown, her traveling clothes and her toiletries.

The cards that Matthew had accidentally left behind were carefully tucked into a corner of her suitcase. Every night she'd played solitaire with them. Maybe that was pathetic, but handling the cards made her feel a little closer to him, and she missed him more than she ever would have thought she'd miss anyone.

Getting back into her routine at home would help, but she didn't kid herself that she'd be over him in no time. She wasn't sure if she'd ever be over Matthew, but being at the ranch with all its memories of him definitely made things worse for her.

She washed the sheets and was planning to clean the bathroom and vacuum, but Pete Beckett had finally talked Sarah into hiring a housekeeper. Keri, a cheerful brunette about Aurelia's age, insisted on handling the final cleanup of Mary Lou's apartment.

Aurelia was upstairs when she heard Sarah call out "They're here!" Aurelia bounded down the stairs, eager to hear how her aunt had survived the trip. She expected woeful tales of the rigors of travel. Aurelia's mother, Mary Lou's sister, had asked for a full report on just how bad the experience had been.

Mary Lou came through the door glowing with happiness. She'd acquired a tan, and she'd never looked better. Even her hair was styled differently. Watkins and Jack followed with the suitcases, and there were several of them.

Watkins, a barrel-chested man with a handlebar mustache, beamed at everyone. "Great trip," he said. "Outstanding."

Aurelia hugged her aunt and waited for the disclaimer.

It never came. Mary Lou raved about the entire experience. At first Aurelia thought her aunt might just be saying she'd loved the honeymoon to spare her new husband's feelings. But as the family gathered in the living room to hear the details of the trip, Aurelia finally realized that her aunt wasn't faking. She'd had the time of her life.

The homecoming celebration moved into the cocktail hour, which included substantial munchies that Sarah and Aurelia had made instead of a formal sit-down dinner. Soon the living room was packed with all ages, from the seven teenagers in residence to the members of the Chance family, including the two Chance grandchildren: Sarah Bianca, a toddler who was into everything, and Archie was still a baby who hadn't yet begun to crawl.

It was bedlam, but a happy kind of bedlam. For the first time since Aurelia had arrived, all members of the family were together, and the chaos helped her forget, for a little while, that she had a permanently broken heart. Much of the talk centered on Jack's half brother Wyatt and the wedding coming up at the end of August.

Wyatt's father and twin brother, Rafe, had promised to come, but Diana, mother to Wyatt and Rafe as well as Jack, hadn't committed. Aurelia hoped to get time off so she could help with the cooking. She was intensely curious about a woman who could run off to San Francisco and leave a toddler behind. Besides, thinking about Jack, Wyatt, Rafe and Diana distracted her from her own troubles.

Then Mary Lou found a moment to draw her into a corner of the room, away from the chaos. "What's this I hear about you and the horse trainer?"

So much for forgetting about Matthew. Aurelia felt her cheeks grow warm. "It was nothing, Aunt Mary Lou. A temporary fling. I promise I didn't let it interfere with my job. In fact, Matthew helped me improve my job performance."

"Heavens, Aurelia, I'm not worried about whether he kept you from doing your job. I know you better than that. But what happened? Everyone thought you two made the perfect couple, and then bam, it was over."

"We aren't right for each other. He's a world traveler, and I'm not into that. It would never have worked out with me wanting to stay home and him constantly on the go."

Mary Lou's eyes narrowed. "You sound *exactly* like your mother."

Aurelia was taken aback by her aunt's tone. "Not surprising, I suppose. She is the one who gave birth to me."

"And passed on the prejudices that we inherited from your grandparents. One bad train trip, and they refused to travel ever again."

"But then my parents ended up in a burning hotel room."

Mary Lou shrugged. "Stuff happens."

"And don't forget my aunt and uncle's horrible car trip to St. Louis."

"Those two." Mary Lou rolled her eyes. "I swear they still subscribed to the flat-earth theory. They thought if they traveled too far in one direction, they'd fall right off. Plop. Done."

Aurelia glanced at her aunt's empty wineglass and concluded that her aunt's tongue might be a little looser than usual. "You don't seem to subscribe to the flat-earth theory."

"Not anymore, but I was a card-carrying member until Watkins dragged me on to this cruise." She wagged a finger at Aurelia. "You've been sold a bill of goods, niece of mine. Travel is *great*."

"Really?"

"Really. I can't believe all the years I've wasted thinking there was nothing worth seeing that required a plane ride, or a train ride or a boat ride. It's a smorgasbord out there, Aurelia, and if you have someone who's offered you a seat at the table, you need to grab that chair."

"But…but, I'd have to quit my job, and get a passport and sublet my apartment, and—"

"Details. Does he want to take you with him?"

"Yes." He'd begged her, in fact.

"Then you would be a fool not to accept, Aurelia Imogene. Can you still get ahold of him, or has he gone off on another trip?"

"He said I could call his cell." Aurelia's heart kicked into high gear. "Sarah has the number."

"Then what the hell are we waiting for, girl?" Mary Lou raised her voice. "Sarah, can you get this horse-trainer fellow on the phone? My niece needs to talk to him."

Sarah looked startled, but she put down her wine immediately and headed down the hall toward her bedroom. "Come with me, Aurelia," she called over her shoulder. "I'm sure you'd like a little privacy, so make the call from my room."

"He's probably left the country by now," Aurelia said as she caught up with Sarah. "I might wake him up if he's in Europe somewhere."

Sarah walked into her bedroom and picked up the cell phone lying on her nightstand. "If he feels about you the way I think he does, he won't mind if you wake him up." She pushed a couple of buttons and handed the phone to Aurelia. "It's ringing. Good luck." Then she walked out of the room.

Aurelia barely had time to take stock of her surroundings, an elegant room furnished in greens and browns, before Matthew answered.

"Sarah?" he said. "Is there a problem with Houdini?"

"It's not Sarah." Aurelia's heart beat so loudly she hoped she'd be able to hear him over it. "It's me."

"Aurelia?"

"Did I wake you? I have no idea where you are, and I—"

"I'm in Jackson."

"Jackson, *Wyoming?*"

"Yeah." His voice was soft and very warm. "I knew you were leaving tomorrow, and I hoped…" He took a deep breath. "I hoped to hear from you before you left."

"You're in Jackson?" She still couldn't quite comprehend that. She'd been so certain he'd be out of the country by now.

"I'm sitting in a restaurant eating a meal that doesn't hold a candle to anything you've fixed."

"Did you want to finish it, or…would you consider…"

"I'm on my way." The line went dead.

Aurelia's hands shook so much she was afraid she'd drop Sarah's phone. She laid it on the polished dark wood of the nightstand and wrapped her arms around her body to try and stop the trembling. He was coming back. She had another chance.

Knowing he'd hung around waiting in case she changed her mind loomed huge. He hadn't written her off and gone about his life. He'd stayed in hopes that she'd reconsider.

She'd read his book and knew he was tenacious when it came to working with horses. Apparently he was tenacious when it came to wooing her. And that's what he was doing, wooing her. She was being pursued by a man who could have any number of women simply by snapping his fingers. But he wanted her.

Head spinning, she walked back down the hall. At the curved staircase she paused, longing to go upstairs, away from the crowd of people, while she waited for Matthew.

Sarah must have been watching for her, because she excused herself from the group and hurried over. "Did you get him?"

Aurelia nodded.

"And?"

"He's in Jackson. He's driving back here."

Sarah's face lit up. "That's wonderful. I'm so glad you called him." She paused, as if considering. "Go wait for him on the porch. You'll have more privacy there."

Aurelia sighed with relief. "Thank you, Sarah."

"What's going on?" Mary Lou walked up next to Sarah. "Did you get in touch with that horse trainer?"

"Yes, I did."

"He was in Jackson," Sarah added. "He'll be here soon."

"That's great." Mary Lou lifted her wineglass. "Well done, niece of mine. Well done."

"Aurelia's going to wait for him out on the porch."

"Good idea," Mary Lou said. "I'll sit with her, keep her company."

"Oh, that's okay, Aunt Mary Lou," Aurelia said quickly. "I'll be fine out there on my own."

"No, you won't," Mary Lou said. "You'll be jittery as a June bug. I'll refill my wine and bring you one. You go ahead. I'll be right there." She took off.

Aurelia glanced at Sarah.

"She's a force of nature." Sarah gazed after Mary Lou. "I've known her for almost thirty years, and I've never felt as if I had the upper hand. You might as well go along with her plan."

"All right, but when Matthew gets here, she'll need to make herself scarce."

Sarah laughed. "When Matthew gets here, you won't even notice that Mary Lou's around."

Moments later, Aurelia sat in one of the porch rockers with a glass of wine and her aunt beside her giving advice about men.

"Don't go along with whatever they dream up," Mary Lou said, "but keep in mind that sometimes they actually might have a good idea. I would never have taken a cruise because our family's been conditioned not to travel, but am I glad Watkins insisted. We're already making plans for the next one."

"But what if I'm not like you? What if I hate traveling?"

Mary Lou patted her arm. "Honey, men who like to travel make great lovers. You won't hate traveling if you're getting some every night."

"Aunt Mary Lou!"

"I'm just sayin'."

"So what are you girls doing out here?" Watkins came through the door with a beer bottle in his hand.

"Girl talk," Mary Lou said.

"Nice out here." Watkins sat down in the rocker next to Mary Lou's. "No wonder you wanted to sit outside."

"Hey, where's the bridegroom?" Jack Chance appeared on the porch. "Oh, there you are. What're you doing out here?"

"It's a nice night," Watkins said.

"It is," Jack said. "Think I'll sit a spell, too." He took the rocker next to Watkins.

When Jack's wife, Josie, came out holding little Archie and looking for Jack, Aurelia had to bite her lip to keep from laughing. The parade continued like that, until the porch rockers were full and the buzz of conversation melded with the chirp of crickets.

"This is nice," Mary Lou said.

"Yes, it is," Aurelia agreed. She wasn't sure how Matthew would react to the welcoming committee, but knowing him, he'd roll with it.

Eventually headlights appeared on the road leading to the ranch.

"I think that's him!" Jack called out. "He made damned good time, too. He might've beat my record."

"Maybe he's better at spotting the cops than you are," said his youngest brother, Gabe, the father of little Sarah Bianca.

"I've framed all my speeding tickets," Jack said. "I consider them a badge of honor, a testament to my manhood."

"I consider them a testament to your inability to locate the fuzz before they locate you," Gabe said.

The teasing grew more raucous about the time that Matthew pulled into the parking area to the far left of the house. Aurelia wasn't sure whether to stay where she was or go meet him in the parking area. She started to get out of her rocker.

Mary Lou put a hand on her arm. "Let him come to you, sweetie," she murmured.

"But everybody's sitting on the porch like some kind of reception line. He has to run the gauntlet."

"From the way everyone's talked about him, he can handle it."

"You're probably right." She remained seated.

Matthew approached the house. She could see the moment he noticed that the porch was filled with people, because he hesitated for a split second. Then he straightened his shoulders and continued toward her.

At the bottom of the steps, he stopped and took off his hat. "Good people of the Last Chance," he said, as if beginning a speech.

"That's us!" Jack called out. He'd obviously been enjoying his beer. "How're you doing, Matthew?"

"Not so good," Matthew said. "It seems that I've lost my heart to a certain Aurelia Imogene Smith."

Aurelia gasped. She would never have guessed he'd make a public declaration like that.

"Does that mean you've come for her?" Jack asked.

"Yes," Matthew said. "If she'll have me."

Jack rocked forward and leaned over to peer down the line of chairs. "You want this son-of-a-gun, Aurelia? Because if you don't, we can run him off. We have the manpower to do it."

"Or the womanpower," Mary Lou said.

"I want him." She stood on shaky legs, put her wineglass on the porch floor, and walked down the steps toward Matthew. She looked into his eyes. "I'd follow this man anywhere."

Amidst cheers and wolf whistles, Matthew smiled and pulled her into his arms. "I'm really glad about that, because I love you, Aurelia. I should have told you so before."

"I wouldn't have believed you before." She wrapped her arms around his neck. "But I do now."

"So is it mutual?"

"Extremely mutual. I think I've loved you from the minute I saw you."

"And I've loved you all my life." He held her close. "It just took me forever to find you." He kissed her then, amid cheers and catcalls from the porch sitters. But as Sarah had predicted, Aurelia forgot that anyone else was even there.

* * * * *

COMING NEXT MONTH from Harlequin® Blaze™
AVAILABLE JULY 24, 2012

#699 FEELS LIKE HOME
Sons of Chance
Vicki Lewis Thompson
Rafe Locke has come to the Last Chance Ranch for his brother's wedding, but he's not happy about it. After all, Rafe is a city slicker, through and through—until sexy Meg Seymour *shows* him all the advantages of going country....

#700 BLAZING BEDTIME STORIES, VOLUME VIII
Kimberly Raye and Julie Leto
Join bestselling authors Kimberly Raye and Julie Leto as they take you to Neverland—that is, *Texas*—in these two sizzling stories, guaranteed to make you want to do anything but sleep.

#701 BAREFOOT BLUE JEAN NIGHT
Made in Montana
Debbi Rawlins
Travel blogger Jamie Daniels is determined to show sexy cowboy Cole McAllister that she's not like all the other girls—in and out of bed.

#702 THE MIGHTY QUINNS: DERMOT
The Mighty Quinns
Kate Hoffmann
With just a bus ticket and $100 in his pocket, Dermot Quinn sets out to experience life as his immigrant grandfather had—penniless and living in unfamiliar surroundings. So the last thing he expects is to strike it rich with country girl Rachel Howe.

#703 GUILTY PLEASURES
Tori Carrington
Former Army Ranger turned security expert Jonathon Reece always gets the job done. This time, his assignment is to bring in fugitive-from-justice Mara Findlay. Too bad the sexy bad girl outwits him at every turn...including in bed.

#704 LIGHT ME UP
Friends with Benefits
Isabel Sharpe
Imagine walking into a photography studio run by the sexiest man you've ever seen and finding pictures...all of you. Jack Shea has captured her essence, but is Melissa Weber ready to bare even more?

You can find more information on upcoming Harlequin® titles, free excerpts and more at www.Harlequin.com.

HBCNM0712

REQUEST YOUR FREE BOOKS!
2 FREE NOVELS PLUS 2 FREE GIFTS!

red-hot reads!

YES! Please send me 2 FREE Harlequin® Blaze™ novels and my 2 FREE gifts (gifts are worth about $10). After receiving them, if I don't wish to receive any more books, I can return the shipping statement marked "cancel." If I don't cancel, I will receive 6 brand-new novels every month and be billed just $4.49 per book in the U.S. or $4.96 per book in Canada. That's a saving of at least 14% off the cover price. It's quite a bargain. Shipping and handling is just 50¢ per book in the U.S. and 75¢ per book in Canada.* I understand that accepting the 2 free books and gifts places me under no obligation to buy anything. I can always return a shipment and cancel at any time. Even if I never buy another book, the two free books and gifts are mine to keep forever.

151/351 HDN FEQE

Name   (PLEASE PRINT)

Address   Apt. #

City   State/Prov.   Zip/Postal Code

Signature (if under 18, a parent or guardian must sign)

Mail to the **Reader Service:**
IN U.S.A.: P.O. Box 1867, Buffalo, NY 14240-1867
IN CANADA: P.O. Box 609, Fort Erie, Ontario L2A 5X3

Not valid for current subscribers to Harlequin Blaze books.

Want to try two free books from another line?
Call 1-800-873-8635 or visit www.ReaderService.com.

* Terms and prices subject to change without notice. Prices do not include applicable taxes. Sales tax applicable in N.Y. Canadian residents will be charged applicable taxes. Offer not valid in Quebec. This offer is limited to one order per household. All orders subject to credit approval. Credit or debit balances in a customer's account(s) may be offset by any other outstanding balance owed by or to the customer. Please allow 4 to 6 weeks for delivery. Offer available while quantities last.

Your Privacy—The Reader Service is committed to protecting your privacy. Our Privacy Policy is available online at www.ReaderService.com or upon request from the Reader Service.

We make a portion of our mailing list available to reputable third parties that offer products we believe may interest you. If you prefer that we not exchange your name with third parties, or if you wish to clarify or modify your communication preferences, please visit us at www.ReaderService.com/consumerchoice or write to us at Reader Service Preference Service, P.O. Box 9062, Buffalo, NY 14269. Include your complete name and address.

He was looking for adventure…and he found her.

Kate Hoffmann

brings you another scorching tale

With just a bus ticket and $100 in his pocket, Dermot Quinn
sets out to experience life as his Irish immigrant grandfather
had—penniless, unemployed and living in the moment.
So when he takes a job as a farmhand, Dermot expects he'll
work for a while, then be on his way. The last thing he expects
is to find passion with country girl Rachel Howe, and his
wanderlust turning into a lust of another kind.

THE MIGHTY QUINNS: DERMOT

Available August 2012 wherever books are sold!

Montana. Home of big blue skies, wide open spaces...and really hot men! Join bestselling author Debbi Rawlins in celebrating all things Western in Harlequin® Blaze™ with her new miniseries, MADE IN MONTANA!

Read on for a sneak peek of
BAREFOOT BLUE JEAN NIGHT

"OVER HERE," Cole said.

Jamie headed toward him, her lips rising in a cheeky grin. "What makes you think I'm looking for you?"

He drew her back into the shadows inside the barn. "Then tell me, Jamie, what are you looking for?"

A spark had ignited between them and she had the distinct feeling that tonight was the night for fireworks—despite the threat of thieves. The only unanswered question was when.

"Oh, I get it," she said finally. "You're trying to distract me from telling you I'm going to help you keep watch."

He lowered both hands. "No, you're not."

"I am. Rachel thinks it's an excellent idea."

He shot a frown toward the kitchen. "I don't care what my sister thinks. You have five minutes, then you're marching right back into that house."

She wasn't about to let him get away with pulling back. Not to mention she didn't care for his bossiness. "You're such a coward."

"Let's put it this way..." He arched a brow. "How much watching do you think we'd get done?"

She flattened a palm on his chest. His heart pounded as hard as hers. "I see your point. But no, I won't be a good little girl and do as you so charmingly ordered."

"It wasn't an order," he muttered. "It was a strongly

worded request. I have to stay alert out here."

"Correct. That's why we'll behave like adults and refrain from making out."

"Making out," he repeated with a snort. "Haven't heard that term in a while." Then he caught her wrist and pulled her hand away from his chest. "Not a good start."

"It's barely dark. No one's going to sneak in now. Once we seriously need to pay attention, I'll be as good as gold. But I figure we have at least an hour."

"For?"

"Oh, I don't know…" With the tip of her finger she traced his lower lip. "Nothing too risky. Just some kissing. Maybe I'll even let you get to first base."

Cole laughed. "Honey, I've never stopped at first base before and I'm not about to start now."

Don't miss BAREFOOT BLUE JEAN NIGHT
by Debbi Rawlins.

Available August 2012 from Harlequin® Blaze™
wherever books are sold.